Myria Personas

One Girl, Some Narratives, Many Lessons

Vandita Mishra

INDIA • SINGAPORE • MALAYSIA

Notion Press

No.8, 3rd Cross Street, CIT Colony,
Mylapore, Chennai, Tamil Nadu – 600004

First Published by Notion Press 2020
Copyright © Vandita Mishra 2020
All Rights Reserved.

ISBN 978-1-64850-712-0

Inspired by real-life stories

For every woman who is fighting her battle...
For every man who is standing strong with her...
And vice versa!

PREFACE

There was a time when I used to laugh at people who always spoke about things revolving around women. What is the need to talk so much about it? I used to think. It wasn't until I faced my own set of problems and struggles that I started taking the big and small conversations about womanhood seriously. Because it was only then that I realised the myriad of complexities that can be associated with this one human gender.

After having started my own journey of exploring this vast way of life, I took a long pause. Thus, it took me longer than usual to finish writing these stories. The pause was partly because of my inner struggles and partly because of the intricacies that surround womanhood. Each time that I was with all of these women that I have written about, I used to be in a different zone altogether. There were times when I enjoyed and connected with them, and there were also times when I couldn't even empathise with their situations.

Though it wasn't easy, this journey made me unravel my own self to a great extent. Thus, I present to you these myriads of personas, some that you will be able to relate with and others that you will be able to learn from. In the end, there is a lot that you will take back with you. Thank you for picking up my book. I will look forward to hearing from you after you finish reading it!

– Vandita

Acknowledgements

This is the most special section of the book for me because it gives me an opportunity to pour out my feelings for the special people behind the book.

I extend my heartfelt thanks to all those women who shared their stories with me. There were instances when it wasn't easy for them, and there were also instances when they had to revise their difficult past while talking to me. But, they still stood strong, because they knew their stories could make a difference. I salute each one of them for their journeys.

Though this book revolves around women and womanhood, I could write it only because of one man who constantly stood behind me. I can't thank Parijat, my strongest pillar, enough for his time to listen to me narrate everyday and for his extremely valuable inputs.

I am thankful to my parents for their constant support and trust in me.

A special thanks to my dear readers for picking up this book. It is you who make me write more and write better.

– **Vandita**

PROLOGUE

Nothing stays the same forever. Not even our own thoughts and opinions. The ever-changing world around us stimulates us to rethink, and our ever-growing intelligence and experience keep us dynamically connected to the external world.

I never thought I would start liking sweet food after a certain age. I never knew I wouldn't remain as disciplined as I was while in college. I never anticipated that I would become pretentious like most people in this world, and I never imagined I would start looking at womanhood so differently.

CHAPTER 1

HOW IT ALL BEGAN...

As a young girl, I had always looked forward to getting married. I was also one of those little girls who loved dressing up; dazzling earrings, bangles, *bindis* and traditional Indian attire were always my favourite things. I never understood why girls cried while leaving their houses during their wedding. "Isn't it supposed to be a new beginning? Why begin something with tears?" I used to think. But as I grew up more, and people and friends around me started tying the knot, even their normal experiences and narratives shook me from inside. I observed my female friends changing drastically after their weddings, and more so after they had children. Their relations with me or people around them were not the same, their work profiles kept going down and were ultimately not a priority anymore, they appeared restricted, caged and confined. "I will take some more time," the scared me used to tell my parents, and I thus ended up delaying my wedding till two years after my post-graduation; after which I gave up and finally got married. This girl who got married by the time she was thirty was much different from the carefree girl in her teens and twenties. Irrespective of who my husband was, how my in-laws were and what my circumstances were, marriage for me was no more a beautiful new beginning. I now looked at it as something which I had to survive. In a constant pursuit to protect my identity and save myself from changing, I was now rebellious towards every little thing. This internal rebel never allowed me to accept my husband completely and made me live half of what I could have lived then.

Professionally, I was a techie and an MBA and was never interested in working for a corporate company. I had worked in one for two years at the start of my career and I had started feeling purposeless during that time. Nine to six and back home was what my life had become. I want to do more with my life than just making marketing strategies for a random company, is what I used to think. Thus, marrying a man settled in Allahabad (now Prayagraj) was a decision that I had made by my own choice. I knew that the town that I was moving to didn't have any corporate companies which would absorb me, but I was very confident about my startup, which was an educational app for board exam students. It was the failure of my startup that had aggravated the rebel in me more. Because it was then that I had started feeling professionally decayed. *If I were a man, I could have changed this decision of settling here,* I used to think. I could have moved to a bigger city and tried other things. I started feeling stuck and suffocated, and with this professional fall, I dragged my personal life along. I didn't want to have children, I stopped supporting my husband when he was in a problem, I thought of getting divorced and I started imagining my life in ten other different ways. I just didn't want to behave and even feel like a woman, because I thought I was cursed to be one. With this slow dissociation from self, I felt terrible each day.

Am I supposed to keep my priorities second to my husband's? Am I supposed to adjust to things that I may not like? Am I supposed to change my identity to something else, just because I am married now? Am I supposed to stay quiet in order to be considered good? Am I supposed to be the giver? The one who relentlessly does it all in order to make others' lives comfortable, irrespective of what they may be going through themselves!

I now had a million such questions in my mind. But I wasn't sure if I was the only one who felt like this. I wasn't sure if my questions were right or wrong. I wasn't sure if more questions existed, the ones which I wasn't aware of. I was hungry to discover more about womanhood. I was craving to know how other women survived this difficult journey. I wanted to know their stories and bring them to the fore; I wanted to understand what being a woman actually meant.

"Sid," I told my husband one day, "I am heading to Delhi for the next one week," and embarked upon this journey which was waiting to show me many more colours of womanhood, more than the ones I had ever known.

CHAPTER 2

Naina

"That's it! I have to get it somehow; this would uplift my profile so much!" exclaimed Naina staring into her phone, which she anyhow was doing most of the time during our conversations. "Sorry, what?" I asked, assuming that she was trying to tell me about something.

"Arrr! Nothing, there hasn't been anything great on my resume for almost three months now. Look here," she showed me her phone. "This is a forum which features women and their stories; they are organising a conference next month. It would be great if I get to deliver a talk here."

"Oh okay, yes, you should try," I smiled.

I had spoken to Naina about a week back. She was sweet and approachable unlike how I thought she would be. I had told her that I was a writer and wanted to meet her in reference to something that I was writing. She had agreed almost immediately and moreover, invited me to her place so that we could get to know each other. Keeping aside what I was feeling about women then, I guess womanhood has been the topic of talks, debates and discussions since forever. And why shouldn't it be? The maximum complexities, variations, restrictions and social changes occur around a woman. From living two different lives, one before and one after she gets married, to leaving everything aside to bear and nurture a child, it's a woman who has the capability of shaping and reshaping herself as per the demands of both nature and her surroundings. It's not for no reason that nature has bestowed such a huge responsibility of being the flag bearer of continuing the human race onto her. Besides all the physical and circumstantial dynamics that she goes through, there is a huge emotional component which is added on to her life by her surroundings. This emotional dynamic that she faces come in the form of challenges given to her by the society and at times by her own near and dear ones.

A hard worker, Naina was someone that I had easily spotted on social media because of her trending posts. She was happily married, had a five-year-old son and was a total enthusiast at work. Naina, who was a certified medical practitioner and a specialist gynaecologist professionally, ran her own little centre where she trained children with special needs; she had started it a couple of years back after having realised the need to have such a friendly learning centre for these children.

"The entire concept of motivational talks has become more like a business, you see," she continued to speak staring into a blank space. "People want to work later and motivate others first, or maybe because you can't do it yourself, you want to be the guru who preaches others to do it."

Wow, okay, she was intense and I was worried where this conversation was headed! I neither wanted to agree nor disagree with this. Well, that ways, yes, I am quite a diplomatic woman myself, which is more so because I feel it's better to stay away from arguments until of course it's absolutely mandatory or you know the other person way too well. Naina could be saying that just because she wasn't in a great mood, so I kept quiet and uttered just a little harmless, "Hmmm..."

"Well, but this forum that I am talking about is a media event. They do their research well, pick some women who are doing different things and invite them formally to deliver a talk," she now appeared calm. "You may think why I am getting impatient about it. But well, that, my dear, is because our world has become like this. No matter what you do, you have to keep yourself active on such forums and of course on social media in order to connect to more and more people for the work that you are doing. I really want more people to know about children with special needs and about how it's absolutely all right for someone to have syndromes and such needs," she appeared to control her tears when she said that.

"Oh yes, I understand that completely," I smiled to make things normal, "and you will make it, you are doing so many things and you are doing them so well," I smiled again. "In fact, I have been stalking your profile and was dying to meet you and speak to you for so long!" She kept her hand on mine lightly, laughed, took both our finished coffee mugs in her hand, said "You are a sweetheart to say that," and disappeared into the kitchen.

While she was away, I looked around the house. It looked like a small apartment which was kept way too neatly. The cosy drawing room where I was sitting connected to the kitchen space, which overlooked a window; outside one could see the other houses of the apartment and a small park which was crowded by small children and their nannies who carried them around. A portion of the kitchen, where the slab and drawers were, was hidden from the drawing room and the partial portion that was visible had a small round dining table to accommodate four people comfortably. Four was exactly the number of residents that stayed in that house-Naina, her husband, their son and her mother-in-law. I was surrounded by a lot of crafty things in the drawing room. A beautiful table lamp hung over the side table next to me, which added to the décor of the room both by the way it looked and by the effect of the light it emitted. I could partially see Naina opening and closing the refrigerator again and again from behind the curtains that were tied by a light string near the dining table. It was five o'clock in the evening and from the sounds and movement that I heard, I assumed that she was preparing some quick evening snack for her son whom she said would return from his friend's house in a bit. I almost got up to peep inside so that I could continue my conversation and make a move before she got busy with the family when her mother-in-law appeared from inside.

"Hello, *beta*! You must be Tanya, I guess," she smiled.

"Oh, hello, Aunty. Yes, I am Tanya. I am glad you know me," I smiled back.

"Yes, Naina was mentioning about you the other day, she told me you would be visiting the house," she sat down slowly and continued to scan me from top to bottom. She did it quickly enough so that it didn't look purposeful but then I got the vibes anyways. I am sure any lady gets an *I am getting scanned vibe* the moment someone looks at them with that intention. I wasn't wearing any of those married women accessories like the toe ring or the nuptial thread, and for a second I wondered if she was getting judgemental about it, but well, she wasn't my mother-in-law and I decided not to pay heed to it.

"Yes, Ma, that's Tanya," Naina appeared from the kitchen. She was holding bread and a knife with some jam on it in her hand. I knew I was right; she was preparing some snacks for her son.

"Naina told me you are a writer," she said.

"Yes, Aunty, I write. I am working on a book right now," I smiled again.

"That's very nice," she said. "Being a writer is a good thing for the ladies. You must be staying at home most of the time, isn't it?"

"Yes, Aunty, I do stay at home most times, except when I have to meet people, attend literature fests or book fairs, etc."

"That's wonderful, running around for a woman in a metropolitan city like this can be very hectic. The family gets overlooked. I am a science graduate myself, but I never preferred to work and run around. I had to bring up two daughters, a son and look after my husband and so many things at home," she looked very convinced with what she was saying.

Naina's family stayed in Delhi, running around in the city could have been challenging but wasn't sitting at home more difficult, I thought. More so in a metropolitan city where most people were confined to their houses and nowadays their phones, unlike smaller towns where women of a colony ganged up and people were at least aware of the who is who of most people in the town.

"When Naina and Sandeep got married, I had told her the same thing. I told her that she would be taken care of by him and she doesn't need to worry about the bills of the house. Sandeep works very hard," her eyes lit up when she said that, "he takes very good care of all of us." Naina appeared again with medicine and a glass of water for her mother-in-law, they smiled at each other and she disappeared into the kitchen, again paying the least attention to our conversation. She had her medicine and continued.

"I have diabetes actually, and if I stand for too long then my back starts hurting. That's why I am not able to do much household work nowadays. A few years back when Naina had just got married, I used to do all the work at home," she sighed. "She being a gynaecologist was unusually busy all the time. I used to tell them to plan their pregnancy early but they delayed and now we all are suffering," she said, adjusting her hair. I felt awkward to hear the word suffering. I wasn't sure why she said that but I just hoped she never said that to Naina. "Now she is busier than before," she continued. "She thinks she can change the way people think about diseases. Poor Sandeep gets ignored and ends up managing many of his meals alone," she was adjusting her sari this time.

"Sorry to keep you waiting," Naina came, gave me a bowl of fruits and sat on the sofa right opposite me.

Her mother-in-law got up and said, "Okay, I will go for a quick bath, it's very hot today," and went inside.

Soon after, the doorbell rang and a lady who appeared to be someone from the neighbourhood walked in with a child. The child bid her goodbye and happily came and sat with us.

"That must be your son," I said.

"Oh yes, that's Nikhil, Nikku my darling," she hugged him and planted a tight kiss on his hair. Nikhil waved a distant and shy hello to me, and I couldn't help but observe that he looked different from most of us. His face appeared broader than usual and was chubby in such a way that I couldn't distinguish his neck below. His eyes looked sleepy and he wore big framed spectacles over them; his nose which was flat looked cute, and he constantly tried to lick his lips with his tongue, which added some naughtiness to it. He smiled at me like no one else ever had; there was a strange sense of genuineness in his smile. Naina fed him with the sandwich and fruits and gave him a quick drawing task which then kept him busy.

"I have delivered many babies, Tanya," she looked away and spoke, "and I had taken all the precautions that I could for my own pregnancy. I was very excited about it, and I used to imagine how it would be to hold my own child in my hands. That day when I held him for the first time, a sudden sense of ecstasy and agony crept over me. My mother-in-law, who is ignorant of medical science, pointed out how broad his face was but I knew it was Down's syndrome. There are specific tests done during pregnancy that detect whether the child in the womb is syndromic or not, and I, of course, had got all possible tests done. But there are a few unfortunate percentages of people where the tests are falsely negative. The chemicals miss what's lying underneath," she was quiet.

Later that evening, I bonded with Nikhil. We drew mountains and the sun together, and we even made some disfigured structures with building blocks. He was adorable in his own unique way. Finally, when I got up to leave, he allowed me to leave with great difficulty and with a promise that we will meet again soon. Naina said she would meet me the next day at her academy and I returned to the guest house which I had booked for my week-long stay in Delhi.

While on my way back, I had mixed thoughts. I thought about Naina's busy profession. I thought what must have driven her to start the academy, what it would be like to be a strong mother to a child who was *syndromic*, or in kinder words *special* and different from the rest. I thought about her mother-in-law, I thought about Nikku. And oh yes, somewhere in the background I was thinking about their neatly kept apartment as well. The place was simple and so was she, and I had loved it that way. With all that I had heard about Naina, I had imagined her to be everything but homely. But how different can things be from how we imagine them to be, isn't it? I am sure this does happen a lot more often with people ever since we have started living on social media because well, the kind of life that we scroll down on our phones is way different from the kind of life that one actually leads. Funnily, with the multiple thoughts that were running in my mind, I was simultaneously thinking how philosophical I was! To put my rampant thoughts at rest, I plugged in my earphones, rested my head on the door of the car and started observing my way outside. I don't know how life in a metropolitan city would have been for me; the hustle, bustle and rush in big cities had always excited me. I saw these as places full of opportunities, as if anything that one wanted to do was possible here, as if life was easier here, as if my life would have been different here.

The next day, I headed to Naina's academy, which was located near a multispecialty hospital. Just like her house, I got some arty vibes from the academy as well. The building which appeared to have two floors had the look of Flemish bond brickwork from the outside. I loved any construction with a varying pattern of brickwork and got immediate good vibes from the place which I was about to enter. I had reached there at a time when the kids must have still not arrived. I was about to enter the building when a lady wearing a neatly draped sari walked up to me and in a very sweet voice said,

"Ma'am, you must be Mrs Tanya."

"Oh yes, I am," I said, and she ushered me to Naina's office.

Naina was busy typing something on her desktop; the moment we entered, she looked up and greeted me with a smile. I took my seat opposite her and finished a cup of tea until she could attend to me.

"So Tanya, come let us show you around," she said as soon as she finished her work.

We walked outside towards the open play area, which looked more like a big garden.

"This place is ours; it belongs to my husband's side of the family. It was originally a bungalow," she raised her eyebrows and smiled, "but my in-laws had left it long back and shifted to the other side of the city due to some bad memories associated with the house. Technically, I was never brought here after my wedding, it was functioning as a guest house, and their family had given it on rent to somebody who ran it."

"How did you manage to end that?" I asked out of curiosity.

"Well, our circumstances make us do all possible things," she smiled. "I was working in a hospital as a busy gynaecologist before my child's birth. After his birth, I never had the heart to get back to the busy schedule, because that would have left my Nikku deprived of the attention he needed. Somehow my mother-in-law never accepted him as wholeheartedly as she should have; somehow my husband didn't have the patience for him. There was an instance when I had started thinking of returning to work, but at the same time discussions and probabilities of leaving Nikku in a mental health centre cropped up in the family. It was then that I had to take a strong decision because though I loved my work, I loved him more. As I started spending more and more time with him, I realised life was just not easy for a Down's baby in most countries. They have special needs, but their families rarely know what lies in the depth of those special needs. Most people end up either fulfilling their formalities or leading their lives as sufferers. I was determined to take a step for as many such children as I could; I wanted to change the way people think about it. I visited a special care centre for these children in Chicago, learned a lot and came back. After coming back, I clubbed with an organisation for special children in Mumbai to get some of my nurses trained, and today here we are, a team of five of us for ten children. We are also trained in providing them with emergency care since their organs again aren't as cooperative with them as ours. We will grow as more and more people know about us," her smile was priceless.

Soon after the children started pouring in, each of them was accompanied by their mothers. They all looked very similar to Nikku: the same broad face, similar eyes and nose. In my heart, I adored Naina for bringing all of them under one roof. We headed inside to one of the rooms and Nikku, who was already busy playing with one of the nurses there, was elated to see me. The room was full of colourful mats and boxes and within no time the children started settling down on them. Naina addressed each one of them individually and they seemed to be really attached to her. She walked towards me again and started explaining the details of the place.

"These children don't have muscles as toned as other children and they are slower in picking up most skills as well. The little things that you can see around in this room are to improve upon their skills and muscles." She picked up a spinner, which spun on pressing its handle. "Look at this for instance. This catches their eye and motivates them to do more of it."

With that a girl came and pulled Naina's dress, probably asking her to play something with her. I observed the kids involved in the variant activities, some were trying to join puzzles, and some sat in big round plastic tubs and were enjoying the merry go round spins that their nurses gave them. Some didn't look to be in a mood to cooperate with the trainees, who dealt with them patiently. Nikku had got involved with a colleague now and they both were trying to throw some spongy balls inside a tent. Naina had surely found the best way to both spend more time with him and to provide many other such children with their special needs. I now knew her hunger to reach and connect to more people on motivational forums, and on forums that could focus on what she was doing. She just wanted to bring this topic to the fore; she just wanted people to know that these children constituted equally in our society, that these children defined a different normal altogether.

"But how about now?" I probed further. "Do you get to hear any negative remarks for not being able to spend all the time at home, or for not being able to manage things, though I know you are?"

"Ahhh! There is no end to remarks, my dear. We have to end them from entering inside us, but yes, as long as we know we are on the right track."

This time she was looking at me straight in the eye as if trying to tell me that *nothing is impossible if our spirits are high!*

The movement around us suddenly increased and I noticed that the moms who were accompanying their children opened their respective lunch boxes. Naina turned towards me again and said, "It's Saturday, the day when we all bring some home-cooked food and share with each other, come."

"Oh, yes, I know about it. I told you, right? I have been stalking you," I laughed.

The boys, the girls and their caretakers all joined in a big feast together. A small girl threw a piece of tissue that she was holding towards me; her mom gestured that she was inviting me to eat from her box. The abnormal that I was between all of them, I failed to understand her indication. I ate a small piece of guava from their box and felt a strange lump in my throat while swallowing it. I felt some strange heaviness in my heart, but my soul smiled to see how togetherness creates miracles. My soul smiled to see how a mother's love can not just defy the norms laid by the society, but also redefine them.

Since I had met Naina last, I was constantly thinking about the challenges that she would have faced to open the academy. But all of a sudden, all the hurdles which she would have faced on her way and in her personal life appeared minor in front of the happiness that I saw on her face then, which clearly came by giving these children a new direction. She was an example of someone who was confident in her skin and accepted and celebrated life the way it came to her. She was an example of someone who knew how to stand up for herself and possibly for others as well. Unlike me, she was an example of someone who did not let her circumstances bind her or define her. With all that she was, and with everything that she was managing, Sandeep surely shouldn't have much of a problem in managing his dinner and lunches. I smirked thinking about her mother-in-law's remark. I was glad that I started my journey on exploring womanhood with this lady who made me look forward to it with a lot of positivity, but I had no clue what was lying ahead of me. A few days later, after finishing some other things in Delhi, I packed my bags and headed back to my hometown. I clearly knew who I wanted to speak to next.

CHAPTER 3

SUNITA

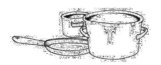

After I returned from Delhi, I was exuding energy. Naina had motivated me to look forward to my subsequent interview sessions with many more women. The best thing was that I had taken the first step of how to approach whom, and I was now more confident in talking to people about their lives. Yes, now that I had taken the first step outside the premises of my house, the next woman that I wanted to know more about was someone who visited my house every day for my daily household chores.

Sunita was almost always late to work, and it was this one thing that annoyed me the most about her because it disturbed my entire schedule. One day though, instead of getting angry at her, I made her sit and asked her why she couldn't ever make it on time. It was then that she had replied to me with teary eyes that she tries her best to reach on time every day, but some or the other problem at her home gets her late. I had taken it lightly and didn't go into the details of her problems then, but I knew that now was the time to know her and her life more closely. The next day after my return, Sunita came at her usual time, rang the bell and said, "Sorry *didi*, I got a little late," as soon as I opened the door.

"Never mind," I said and made way for her to enter inside.

"Thank you, *didi*. I think you are in a good mood today," her smile was wide.

"Oh yes, very! And guess what? I have even made some tea for you today," I said and entered the kitchen.

"Sorry, *didi*," she murmured, thinking that I was sarcastic.

I emerged with two cups of tea from my kitchen and Sunita's mouth was left half-open. "Come, we will sit on the terrace," I said and indicated her to join me.

A surprised Sunita wiped her hands on her sari and followed me outside.

I used to spend at least one hour on my terrace as a part of my daily routine. Except for the horrid lizards that occupied it, the terrace was my favourite portion of the house. Surrounded by some quiet corners and a lot of trees, the only sounds that I heard there were of the wind, the rustling leaves, some birds which chirped every now and then and the peacocks which surrounded our accommodation in plenty. I made Sunita sit with me amidst this serenity that surrounded us. She was still in shock and was just staring at me, while I continued to stare at the leaves above me. After I gathered my thoughts, I spoke.

"So Sunita, I was thinking that though I see you almost daily I don't know you enough. Like how things are at your home, in how many other houses you work, what your children are like, etc." I sipped my tea and gestured her to have some too. She still looked perplexed and took a quick sip from the cup.

"Relax, Sunita," I finally smiled, "I too am a human being like you."

"Yes, *didi*. I am sorry but it's a little overwhelming for me; it's difficult to gather that I am sitting here and having tea with you. Normally, every day I just enter many big houses, clean them, put the things in it back in shape, remove the litter, clear the garbage bins and leave. I am somebody that nobody pauses to speak to because everyone has something more important than me to attend. Unlike the offices which bigger people have, our workplaces do not offer us so much respect. That's why I just ..." she quickly took another sip of tea from her cup to control her tears.

I stood up and started looking around at the trees in order to let her settle and make her more comfortable. She took her time and after a while, came and stood next to me.

"I have three daughters, *didi*. My husband doesn't work; he is bedridden. I have the responsibility of bearing all four of them," she stood quiet for sometime after saying that. "When I got married things were different. He used to work as a security guard in a reputed hotel and was earning decently to support both of us," she took a pause again. "But then," she continued, "after I had my first child, things changed. He used to avoid coming home in order to escape his duties towards our child. He spent most of the nights outside on the streets with his friends and that is where he started having alcohol, which then became his regular habit. I used to handle my infant alone, *didi*. He had no idea about the food and vegetables in the house. Most of the time I used to sit and cry with my daughter, cursing my destiny," she sobbed.

I kept my hand on her shoulder and held it tight. She looked back, smiled at me and continued.

"The women in my neighbourhood had started noticing this; some of them used to come, curse my husband and go, while the others came and showed their sympathy to me. *Didi,* do you know Laxmi? The lady who works in 108, that flat in front?" She pointed out to the flat and asked me.

"The one who rides a bicycle with a big basket in front?" I asked.

"Yes, same," she appeared elated. "Great, *didi*, you also notice so much," she smiled.

I was glad I was able to put a smile on her face.

"So the same Laxmi suggested me to start working in households and earn a living for myself and my daughter," she appeared confident. "I was also tired to rely on my husband, because he used to spend most of his money on alcohol and never cared about us. Thus I started working."

"But your child must have been small, how did you manage that?" I asked her.

"*Didi*, I started with two houses initially and I requested the madam there to allow me to bring my child along. I used to feed her and worked while she slept in a corner in the house. There were days when I wasn't able to pay too much attention at work, but by God's grace I used to manage things."

"Then how about two more children that you have. You said your husband never came home! Did you both continue staying together after all this?" I was curious.

"Yes, *didi*, once I started working he used to come home more often. Instead of giving us support, he came for his own support. He used to take money from me sometimes and I used to give him. This was my mistake."

"But why did you do that? You knew that his habits were not good, right?" I was angry.

"Yes, *didi*, but he said that he was trying to leave alcohol and he just wanted to clear all debts that he had with his friends. Thinking it will all be settled eventually, I used to help him. I didn't know it will land me in deeper trouble. Also, in this duration, I got pregnant twice, and to make things worse I gave birth to two more girl children," she looked away.

"A child is a child, Sunita," I said firmly.

"Yes, *didi*, I know that; we keep hearing all such good things over the radio and TV also, but the reality in our community is very different. A girl child is a liability, we have to get them married and they don't support in our livelihood either," she looked thoughtful.

"Do you guarantee that your sons will support your livelihood Sunita?" I asked her.

She stayed quiet because she knew she couldn't guarantee me that, because she knew life was not as predictable as we thought it was.

"Did having more children make things worse for you then?" I asked again.

She gathered her emotions and continued, "Yes, *didi*, I guess if I would have had a boy, then my husband would have got some hope to look forward to fatherhood, but after them, he openly expressed his aversion and disinterest. Instead of spending nights with his friends, he used to stay home and still be away. He used to return back home in a drunken state and it was me who had to bear with all that he did after that. The good thing was that I didn't leave work. It was difficult for me to manage my daughters but then I got used to it. This continued for almost two years, people around had started suggesting me to leave his house and stay at some other place, and just when I took this seriously and gathered some strength to move out and get completely independent, he met with an accident. He was returning back home from his regular duty one day when he got hit by a truck. Since it happened near our house, people identified him and took him to the government hospital nearby. The doctors said he could have lost his life, but something more unfortunate happened. He got injured in his back and his lower body became lifeless. They said his nerves are damaged and he won't be able to move for the rest of his life!" she was sobbing now.

I had this extremely bad habit of always cribbing and complaining about things around, for which my husband always used to tell me that, *when real problems come you won't be able to do anything about them, as long as you think you are able to do anything in a situation then it isn't a problem at all.* To not able to move your body at your will, even when you wanted to, was certainly a real problem, I thought.

"Calm down, Sunita! You are such a brave lady, and..." I was just trying to utter a few good words to increase her morale when she got a call.

"*Didi*, I am sorry, I got stuck with some urgent work today, please pardon me. I won't be able to come," she said over the phone, after which she made a few more phone calls to the houses where she worked to convey the same.

Sunita was heard by someone outside her community for the first time ever, and that was a reason enough for her to say no to work for a day, I suppose. Sometimes just listening to people with patience extends the maximum help to them. After having spoken to them, she looked at me, smiled and continued again.

"The day he got hit by the truck, he wasn't drunk. He was rather coming home early after ages together. I am not sure why? Maybe he was trying to spend more time with us, maybe he wanted to improve upon his habits or maybe he was just coming home to take some money from me again. I never asked him that. I rather assumed that it was for us that he was returning home. My assumption has made me accept him to date, *didi*. My assumption is what is making me serve him everyday till today," she held my hand and looked at me in relief.

I smiled at her and asked, "Tea?"

"Okay, *didi*," she smiled back.

"Then make some for both of us, madam," I laughed.

Later that day, I requested Sunita to take me to her house; after having heard her, I wanted to see what I had merely visualised. Her house was located right outside the premises of the building where I stayed. Not just her house, the small area next to our building was cramped with many more houses like hers. I had driven past that area many a time before but had never noticed it with the detail with which I noticed it that day. As soon as I entered that area with her, I noticed many eyeballs turning towards me. Draped in a silk kurta pyjama and with spectacles on my eyes, I must have surely looked like an alien there. As I looked around, I could see most children running around in their underclothes. Old plastic bottles and some more litter lay outside one house, which Sunita said belonged to a scrap dealer. I could see crows, dogs and tiny insects hovering all over the place. The houses were placed so near to each other that initially, it was difficult for me to make out whether the adjoining portion was the neighbourhood of a house or an extension of the same house, but as I crossed more houses, I realised that each house was mostly as big as a single room, unlike the huge luxurious houses we had. Sunita's house was located somewhere in between this tunnel-like colony. Painted in a light pink colour and with a tin sheet on the top, it looked very similar to all the other houses in the colony. The area between the four walls was all that Sunita had to accommodate a paralysed husband, who lay in a corner of the house on a charpoy, and three young daughters. She didn't have the privilege of having many rooms for many activities, unlike people in my community, and thus she had designated each corner of the house for separate work. Besides the corner in which her husband lay, the other three corners were for cooking, changing clothes and for her daughters, respectively. Sunita hurried into the house, removed a pile of clothes from a stool, offered me to sit and rushed again to her kitchen corner, probably to get some water. I was overwhelmed by her gesture and fell short of words to even say no to that. I took that time to observe her daughters, the oldest one who must have been seven or eight years old tried to follow her mother in the kitchen, while the other two appeared timid, stood straight and observed me quietly. She brought me a glass of water quickly and insisted me to sit again.

"No, Sunita, I am good," I said and had the water that she offered.

She then introduced me to her daughters who greeted me with a *namaste,* and to her husband who nodded his head in acknowledgement. She told me that her husband was unable to do any of his routine activities by himself and it was she who had to look after all his big and small needs.

"Presently, I work in seven houses, *didi*," she said. "If it was not for all this, I could have easily managed five more houses," she gasped for breath while talking. She appeared excited to have me at her place. She held her eldest daughter and said, "Once this one is a little more mature, she can manage those houses for me and help me," she smiled while her daughter blushed.

There was no point asking if her daughters ever studied or went to school because, with the kind of life that I was looking at where everyday survival itself appeared challenging, education was nowhere a priority. After interacting with her daughters for some time, I asked for her leave and moved out of the house with her. On my way back, she insisted on walking with me till my building. I took this as an opportunity to interact a little more with her, "Sunita, where do you see your daughters in the future?" I asked her.

"*Didi*, where means? They will anyways get married, so I am trying my best to teach them good household work, so that if they get unfortunate like me they can at least manage their lives by working somewhere," she explained.

"Have you ever thought of training them for some other work? Something with which they can make a better living for themselves. And why do they have to get unfortunate to earn, Sunita? They are intelligent little beings who are fortunate to have a brave mother. They should learn to be independent even if they get the best of husbands, shouldn't they?" She blushed and I was glad I could make her blush.

In the subsequent days, I got her daughters enrolled in a government school. She questioned me on the use of getting them enrolled because she could not afford higher education she said. To which I just told her that sometimes it's necessary to take the shorter steps in life in order to unveil the newer paths that may be lying ahead of us.

"Or if you feel it's too philosophical for you to digest, then just know that at least your daughters will get more groomed and learn to interact with people better. Moreover, you can peacefully work while they are at school instead of worrying about them at that hour," I had explained.

I too didn't know till where I could follow them up in future. All that I knew was that I had guided them into some direction then and would continue guiding them further in the next stages of their lives until whichever point I could.

Despite all the hardships that her husband gave her, Sunita was still standing tall by her husband's side. Even if she had to make assumptions in her own mind to look at life in a brighter way, she did it just to make her difficulties more tolerable for her. Why then couldn't I support my husband the way I should have despite him being there by my side in everything that I needed? Why then couldn't I accept my husband wholeheartedly when I knew that it was for me that he rushed back home fast every day? They say there are two types of people, one the more successful and happier ones who learn from others' mistakes and second, the ones who make their own mistakes and choose to go through their own set of hardships. Unfortunately, I fell in the second category, I guess!

CHAPTER 4

NANDINI

After having written about Sunita, I refrained from writing for a very long period of time. Not that I didn't want to, but somehow I just wasn't able to. Always unsatisfied with everything I had, my focus had now shifted from my life to others' lives. I was too preoccupied with comparing my life to that of others to have written anything at all. I used to scroll down profiles on my social media, imagining my life in ten different ways, thinking who will land where in the next ten years and so on and so forth. In an attempt to escape from my negative thoughts, I used to spend my entire day talking to multiple people over the phone for hours together, just to fall trap to their emotions and their lives. I had no time for positive thoughts, I had no time to grow, I had no time to look where I was heading. There were times when I cursed the technology that keeps us connected.

"It would have been so nice if there were lesser means of communication and connectivity," I used to tell my husband often. "With these increasing modes of instant communications and with this facility to post about your personal lives online all the time, we have lost touch with our own lives I feel."

He never used to argue or comment much over it. "It all depends on how you use it!" was all that he always said.

Little was he aware that I was comparing him with others as well. What if I married so and so and my life turned out so and so, my vicious thoughts were endless. It's strange how we can make a mess out of our own lives. I could have had slightly better control over my mind if I had everyday work to attend to, office politics to get involved in and a forced routine to follow, but then there were no options for a techie like me in Allahabad city.

One day while roaming in a supermarket, I came across Nandini. She was someone who was introduced to me by my parents when I had first shifted to Allahabad after my wedding as my father's colleague's daughter, who was married and settled in the same city.

"Hey, long time," I greeted her with her a wide smile and so did she.

"Yes, I guess I am seeing you for the first time in three years," she exclaimed. "Three years right, since you got married?" she asked.

"Almost," I said.

"Children?" she interrogated further,

"Hey no! Didn't plan yet," I answered.

"Why should you do that, Tanya? Kids should have been your priority immediately after you got married. And then what great thing are you doing anyways!"

Wow! Her words pricked me hard. I didn't know we were supposed to plan kids while we were doing nothing great, and I didn't know that was the first thing you asked someone when you were meeting them after long.

"Ooh! I need to rush back home," she looked at her phone and said. "It's my husband's video call. He doesn't know I am outside. He will get angry," she looked worried.

"But you are buying groceries anyways! What's there to get angry in that?" I asked her.

"No, both my kids are at home, he doesn't want me to leave them and go out for any work." "Ooh! You left them alone, is it?" even I was worried now.

"No, no, my mom is there. She has visited us for two days. We also have two full-time caretakers; those are the perks of being an IAS officer's wife, you see," she flaunted.

"Why then can't you step out to buy your groceries?" I was confused.

"I can't explain it now; I am hurrying back home. By the way, save my number. It is..." she gave me her number, paid her bills and rushed outside the supermarket.

Nandini's words had diverted my thoughts for good. Instead of digging for more negativity in my own life, I was now wondering what her life was like. She looked very different from when I had met her last; I wondered what made her change. Before my parents had formally introduced me to her, I remembered seeing her on a couple of occasions in our family get-togethers where she used to visit with her parents. From the short interactions that I had with her back then, I remembered her as a confident and carefree architect who had spoken to me about how she was trying to create some unique designs for smaller homes. As opposed to then, when I saw her now, the confident and carefree Nandini looked more anxious and timid. I was curious to know about her life. Maybe there is something that I can learn from it; maybe there is something that I can write about, I thought, and called her a week later. "Oh! Yes, come down home on Thursday, it has been long due anyways," she said.

"Hi! Nice to see you. I hope you didn't have much problem in locating the house," Nandini greeted me with some warmth as soon as I entered their house.

"No, no, it was rather simple, this community is well known, I guess," I smiled.

"Oh, yes, that's because he was very particular about the location of the house. Our house in Lucknow was huge, and then there were more options for entertainment and activities for children in Lucknow when compared to Allahabad. Thus, when we shifted from there to here, he wanted as many facilities inside the premises of our community as there could be. This is one of the best communities in the city. We have a huge swimming area, gym, shopping complex and what not inside," she was thrilled.

I assumed that *he* here must have been her husband and said, "That's great! And then the perks of a transferable job are the multiple cities one gets to stay in."

"Yes, but they have to work very hard. It isn't easy to work in the Indian civil services, and it isn't easy to get into it either," she laughed, said 'just a moment' and went somewhere inside.

"Tea or coffee?" She appeared again,

"Oh! No, please don't bother yourself with either," I tried being humble.

"No, no, there are many helpers. They will make it, don't worry,"

"In that case, coffee maybe," I said sheepishly.

She instructed her helpers and sat down with me. "I remember speaking to you a few years back at Gupta Uncle's party where you told me about some of your unique ideas of modern interiors for smaller homes. I had just loved them," I started our conversation.

"Oh!" she said, "Architecture! Yes, there are a lot of innovative things that I can plan. I had undertaken one small research, where I visited these houses with an area of approximately four hundred square feet. I assessed the shortcomings in these houses and came up with five innovative strategies. It was much appreciated by our professor," she was lost.

"Well, great! I am sure there may be a lot of houses in our Allahabad itself which can get benefitted by your strategies," I said.

"Ah!" she exclaimed. "Those were student days, Tanya. You could think and do whatever you wanted to. Now I am married. I have a lot of responsibility on my head. I have my husband and kids to look after. Architecture is not my piece of cake anymore. And then my husband is working so hard anyway, all that he wants me to do is to take care of his family life. He relies on me for most of his work. He is like a third child to me," she laughed. I stayed quiet. "Actually, while our wedding was getting fixed, he had told me that he didn't want his wife to work. He says it spoils the decorum of the house, and he is right. Now imagine if I had a full-time career. I wouldn't have been able to teach my kids all the art and craft I teach them during the day time. I wouldn't have been able to feed my husband with hot chapattis and wouldn't have had time to cook every day as well. In western countries, many ladies manage both work and cooking, but Tanya, what do they eat anyway. I am sure most of them get used to eating sandwiches and burgers for lunch," she smirked.

"Well! You are managing your house quite well and it can be seen!" I said looking around.

I didn't agree with many things that she was saying then, but I didn't want to argue with her or question her for anything because I was sure she would have given me some logical explanation that her husband would have fed into her mind for the same. Our conversation was interrupted by a lady who walked into the drawing room. She appeared familiar to me, and before I could ask Nandini said, "That's my mother, do you remember meeting her before?"

"Ah! Yes, I remember seeing her at least," I was honest.

"*Beta*, the kids are asking for their colouring books. I gave them one, but they said mamma gives us a different one. Just check what they want," her mother said to her, and Nandini disappeared somewhere inside. Meanwhile, her mother sat down with me.

"How are you, Aunty?" I smiled.

"I am fine, *beta*. It's very tiring to run around with the kids for the entire day. You don't have children yet?" she asked.

I guess that question runs in the genes of the family, I thought, said no and laughed in my head.

"I am very happy for Nandini," she said looking around. "We were much tensed for her marriage, but then Alok and his family have accepted her well and she is settled now," she expressed further.

"Yes, Aunty, weddings are every parent's concern," I said.

"Actually *beta*, Nandini's complexion has always been an issue. You know right, it's difficult to get good proposals in such cases. You must have also noticed the pockmarks on her cheeks. Three proposals before Alok didn't work out for her for the same reason; thus we decided to compromise a little bit and get her settled. What would she have achieved by working full-time anyways, her husband is taking care of all their needs," she was continuing when I interrupted.

"I didn't get the compromise part, Aunty?"

"*Beta*, they didn't want Nandini to work after her wedding. Alok has a busy job so their family wanted someone who could take care of him and his family. Initially, Nandini was reluctant about that but we made her understand that certain compromises are necessary in life in order to get well settled. If you are working, then I request don't mention much about your work and career to her, because I know somewhere inside she still has that spark to do something in her field. It's better if we don't ignite it, isn't it?" she looked up towards the roof.

How could they think she was flawed? How could she think she was flawed? If we are not confident in our skin and if we don't accept ourselves for what we are, then we end up leading our lives so differently, I thought. We end up accepting things far lesser than what we actually deserve. We end up doing so much injustice to ourselves.

"Slow, slow, slow," Nandini appeared with her kids from inside. "See, she is your *masi*," she told her kids pointing out to me. "Touch her feet quickly."

Both her children came running and touched my feet with a lot of innocence on their faces. They were truly adorable.

"Tanya, now that you know the house, you should join us over the weekend for my daughter's tonsure ceremony; if possible, bring your busy husband along," she said.

"Oh wow! I will be glad to come down, and I will surely try my best to bring him along," I smiled.

"Yes, that's the reason why Ma is staying here for longer. She is helping us with all the arrangements. We have the facility to book a guest house in the government quarters in his name. We have booked the same for her," she said.

All this while I was thinking her mother must be staying with them in the same house, but anyways I thought. After this, I took her leave and promised her to be back that weekend for the ceremony.

"Hey Sid, Sunita is on leave today and I am writing something. I am just too occupied in this to cook dinner. Can we eat a little late, in which case I will finish this segment and try making something quickly," I told my husband because it was eight in the night already.

His full name was Siddharth but I preferred calling him Sid instead.

"Why don't I cook some dinner for you in that case?" he said, "How about biryani and raita? Would you want to have some of that?" he asked and I nodded with a smile.

He was always adorable and supportive, and he understood me very well. After the failure of my startup idea, it was he who had seen the spark of writing in me. He had made me start my blog and kept me motivated enough to keep posting in it. If there was anyone who wanted me to write more and write better, it was him. But then, submerged in negativity, I was always of the thought that he does that selfishly just to keep me confined at home.

***

It was the weekend and I had to visit Nandini again. She called me that morning and informed me to reach by the *ghat* of Sangam River instead of her house for the ceremony.

"I forgot to mention the location the other day," she had said over the call.

I reached well on time to the place directed by her. Instead of occupying just a small area by the riverside for the ceremony like how they usually have in the tonsure ceremonies, Nandini's family had made it a huge affair. They attempted to make a gated entrance for the ceremony area with a small boundary all around, so one could easily identify it as a closed private area on the *ghat*. There were large tents with food stalls and seating arrangement for guests on one side. There were separate stalls for prasad distribution on the other side. A lady draped in a gaudy sari sat on an armchair and was receiving gifts from people who constantly went and either touched her feet or just greeted her and spoke to her. I guessed her to be Nandini's mother-in-law. In the middle of all this stood a slightly elevated platform which was the place for all the action for the day. I spotted a confused and lost Nandini in the middle of it, and went ahead to greet her. She was draped in a shimmery red sari and covered her face till her forehead with a veil. As I neared her, I noticed that she was wearing nearly as many accessories as a bride. The April sun was making her sweat from its heat and the fire from the yajna was adding to it.

"You came?" she said as she turned towards me in a hurry. "But what is this dress that you are wearing?" she appeared angry.

"Sorry, what?" I was offended. I was draped in a light cream and golden salwar kameez. I thought it was perfect for a riverside tonsure ceremony in the month of April.

"You are married, Tanya! You should have worn something in red for the occasion! You aren't wearing your toe rings either," she looked down at my feet and said. "Please step down from this platform. I can't allow you to sit in the yajna like this. It's inauspicious," she said and turned her back towards the priest who probably asked her for something.

For a second, I wanted to walk out of the ceremony, but I stayed. I stayed because I wanted to witness what followed. While I sat in the guest area on one of the chairs in the corner, I observed a carefree Alok roaming around in the yajna area, joking and laughing with some people. I could see Nandini completely involved in the ceremony while she also kept an eye on and handled both her kids simultaneously. Nandini's mother and father sat on the edge of the elevated platform where the yajna was going on. With them, they had few big baskets which probably contained gifts. They were giving those baskets to one person at a time, to those who were brought there by Nandini's father-in-law. While she herself looked anxious and confused, her parents looked submissive and timid in that overall environment. She wasn't being as open with them as a girl should have been with her parents otherwise. What surprised me next was to see her father touching Alok's feet at a point during the prayer ceremony, while Alok stood there in all his glory. I am not sure if it was an important part of their ritual or something which the yajna demanded. All that I knew was that I would have never allowed my father to touch my husband's feet and for how much I knew Siddharth, he would have never allowed him to do so either. Nandini's parents, who had been only distributing gifts throughout the ceremony, were finally giving some precious gifts to Nandini's in-laws' side of the family by the end of the ceremony. If this is what it is like at the tonsure ceremony itself, I thought, then the wedding ceremony would have certainly involved a lot more *compromise* than what I was told about by Nandini's mother.

I was somebody that nobody was bothered about in the ceremony. And for sure I wasn't dressed appropriately enough to meet more of her family members, which I guess could have embarrassed her further. Thus, I quietly made my way out of the pandal and slowly started walking towards my vehicle, which was parked on the outside premises of the riverside. I always used to wonder why certain women are the way they are. For instance, why can't they stand up against the certain wrongs around them, why don't they support empowered women, why do they accept things which they feel are unacceptable, why do they try to drag other women into obsolete things instead of being the change, and why don't they just be themselves! That day I understood that women are not born that way; they don't opt to be that either. They are rather slowly manipulated and trained into being that self that they eventually become. If I looked at Nandini's life from the outside, then it certainly looked great. A respected officer's wife living in a big house with all kinds of help available at her doorstep, who needn't worry about the finances of the house. But at least to me, this picture-perfect life of hers wasn't as perfect from close because despite having everything it lacked her own identity, it lacked the respect she deserved. I still didn't know whether women like Nandini were a victim of their circumstances or they were someone who happily accepted everything that was offered to them. But I certainly knew that by becoming such blind followers of every big and small thing that was taught to them, they were surely responsible for creating many such situations for womanhood which empowered women had to fight for.

CHAPTER 5

SEEMA

Sid came back home slightly upset one day. He looked lost and he was quieter than his usual self. As soon as he came back home, he went inside his room without making any conversation. Having understood that vibe, even I stayed quiet and instead made some tea for us in that duration. After a while, he came and sat in the drawing room with me. While I poured his tea, I casually asked, "How was your day?"

"Life can be so difficult for some people, Tanya! We are so fortunate to be living the way we are," he said. "I mean, as a surgeon I do realise it at many points and on many days but today, in particular, I happened to encounter a young girl and all this while I have been wondering how life can be." He took a pause.

Sid was a general surgeon by profession. He was very passionate about his work and very dedicated to his patients. He belonged to a small village near Allahabad city and thus he had decided to settle and work in that region, so that he could do some good for his people.

"What happened to her?" I asked him.

"She had undergone three surgical procedures on her abdomen previously and today was her fourth. The previous three were for a tumour and today she underwent an abortion," he said, taking a sip from his cup.

Instead of asking anything further about her, "Can I meet her, Sid?" is what I said.

After two days, I accompanied Sid to his hospital. After having crossed a lot of faces with agony, worry and hope on their faces, I finally reached the gynaecology ward where this girl whom Sid had told me about was admitted. He had informed the team of medical and paramedical staff in the hospital about my visit, and since they said that their patient was all right to interact with, I was allowed in her room. Since it could have been awkward to enter her room like a stranger, I took Sid along with me. He had operated on her previously for her tumour; thus she was both friendly and familiar with him. As soon as we entered the room, their family stood up and greeted Sid with a namaste. The small private room that we were in was occupied by the girl and four other people, including two boys, a man and a lady. The man who appeared to be her father came ahead to talk to Sid.

"Sir, actually I wanted to discuss something about her previous reports to you."

"Well, sure," he said, "but before that, I will just introduce you to my wife." He looked at the man and then at the girl and spoke, "She is Tanya, she is a writer and wanted to know if she can speak to you ... Seema," he said, looking at her file which was lying on the table beside her, to probably recollect her name.

There was a small moment of silence in the room; I could see the family exchanging some looks with each other. I took a deep breath, thinking whether I was being intrusive but stayed quiet anyways.

"Of course she can," Seema said, breaking the awkward silence.

We both smiled at each other. The environment of the room now appeared more relaxed. Her father then went out with Sid and returned only a couple of hours later. The boys, who she introduced to me as her brothers, appeared reserved said, "Ma, while she is here with *didi*, we will go and finish the bank work," and left.

"Ma, why don't you go home? Take some rest and come, anyways papa is in the hospital. If I need anything I will call him," Seema said to her mother, about which she initially argued but then left for home.

After Seema and I were left alone in the room, she finally addressed me, "Please make yourself comfortable. Come, you want to sit up with me on the bed instead of that sofa?" she gestured, pointing at the bed.

"Hey, that's very sweet of you, but I am fine here," I was overwhelmed with her gesture.

"No, dear, it's very hard and you have to sit for a little longer, that's why I am saying," she said.

Taking the mid-way, I dragged a plastic chair next to her bed, made myself comfortable by folding my legs up on it and spoke, "Multiple surgeries in the abdomen must not have been easy, have they?" To my surprise, she looked at me and laughed hard.

"How can multiple surgeries be easy, dear!" she exclaimed. "I am sure you are wondering what landed me into an abortion if it was natural, then where my husband is, etc.," she started.

Contrary to the image which I had built about her in my mind, Seema came across as a talkative and charming young girl.

"I will tell you all about it! I have been battling some or the other problem in my body since my childhood. I remember being absolutely all right till I first got my monthly periods at the age of thirteen. Ever since then, things have been just weird and slightly on the challenging end for me."

As soon as she said periods, I was reminded about the time when I had gotten mine. It had started way early at the age of ten for me. I remembered noticing a line of blood on my thigh and I had assumed that I would have got a bad injury somewhere in my stomach. Since I was a naughty kid, I got scared to report it to my mother or anyone else in the family. I thought they would scold me for playing on the streets and jumping around, which I was sure would have caused the wound. The next day in school, I had a weird feeling in my stomach the entire day, and on using the toilet at one point in the break hours, I was shocked to see my panty soaked in blood. It had turned me blank and I had no idea what should have been done about it. I had quietly attended the rest of the session in school. By the time I returned home, the bloodstain had spread all over on the back of my tunic, and I guess one of my aunts noticed it and informed about it to my mother. "So basically every month from now on you will experience this flow of blood from your urinary area. It is a natural process, and every girl experiences this after a certain age," she had explained. "Here," she said, giving me a sanitary pad in hand, "this is what you are supposed to use during these four-five days in the month. Also, try wearing loose, airy clothes," she said, pointing at my favourite *Ruf and Tuf* jeans which I was wearing then. I was a sporty kid and all this that she said had made me feel very heavy at heart. For some reason, I assumed that I would have to restrict wearing jeans, I can't play and run around as much and so on and forth. This little fear in me continued for some months until I got used to this monthly flow and started being my naughty self again.

"So after that age, I started experiencing stomach pain a little more than often," I concentrated back on Seema as she spoke. "One day, it was acute, which got me admitted and treated for appendicitis. It is something which many young adults would have undergone I am sure, but for me, it didn't cure my abdomen entirely. Even after having my appendix removed, the subtle pain in my stomach was maintained. What led me to the hospital again was blood in my stool. The doctor then told me that I had a condition called *ulcerative colitis*. I was given a list of precautions to be followed and was instructed about some dietary restrictions. Besides, there were a series of mandatory tests that the doctor advised me. And those tests, my dear Tanya, led to some further discovery," she laughed again. "Curious to know about it?" she smiled and asked.

I was slightly embarrassed. For a moment, I felt like a hungry storyteller who was sitting in front of a random stranger, making her revise the tough incidences of her life.

"Hey, why do you look lost?" Seema asked, identifying the look on my face.

"Hey, no nothing," I said. "I just hope I am not a disturbance for you here. If you don't feel comfortable at any point, please do let me know. I will quietly take your leave."

"Come on, Tanya! Do you feel that because I am laughing too much?" she asked. "Well, I am laughing because I have cried enough, my dear. Now I am used to the fact that life is a little unfair to me. Life has made a mockery out of me and I am now supporting it by laughing at my woes!" She held my hand.

I wondered who was the sufferer here, me or her. But, her words certainly put my embarrassment to rest and I heard her more peacefully now.

"Yes, so breaking your curiosity, the ultrasound of my big tummy made the doctors find a tumour sitting in my kidney. In some cases, with this *ulcerative colitis* that I have, one can get cancer in the kidneys. But yes, here I got lucky okay, this tumour was discovered at a very early stage and before it could harm any other portion of my body it was removed, thus leading to the second surgery. Should we have some tea on that note, dear?" she asked.

"Oh yes, of course!" said the tea lover in me. "Should I get some from the canteen downstairs?" I asked.

"No, no, you can make it in the kettle kept in that corner," she pointed out.

While I prepared tea, she used the washroom.

"I like what you are wearing by the way. Is this a readymade kurta or you have got this stitched?" she asked.

"I got it stitched. I usually design all my kurtas myself," I said, "And the petite thing that I am, the readymade ones don't fit me at all. So I don't have any other option either."

We both laughed.

"The third surgery," she continued as she took a sip from her mug, "was because the nasty tumour had reappeared after one year, but this was almost five years back dear; I had been stable since then. The diet and checkups were a part of my regular regimen but here I am again!" She exclaimed. "Ask your husband, dear, the doctors love seeing me or what?" She was finally quiet.

"I didn't ask you about your profession," I tried diverting the conversation a little.

"I am a fashion designer. I work in collaboration with a designer in Delhi. I was I mean, working in close collaboration with them," she stammered. "Dr Siddharth must be a great husband, isn't he?" she looked at me and asked.

"Oh what? Yes!" I didn't want to say any word beyond that because somehow, I could see where this conversation was heading.

"How is my brave girl? My darling daughter, how are you doing?" asked Seema's father as he entered the room.

Seema's voice and facial expression changed completely as soon as she saw him. Like a small kid, she jumped straight out of bed and hugged him. He asked her whether she wanted to eat anything, if she was comfortable enough or if she needed anything else.

"Papa, I am absolutely all right. Have you eaten anything? Please eat something. I don't want you to lose weight; you are just perfect at hundred kgs," she said, to which they laughed and her father left again.

"My father has stood by me in the best and worst, Tanya. I am extremely lucky to have him around," she got emotional. "He makes me restore my faith in manhood."

"It is beautiful, the bond that you share with him," I smiled at her.

"I have never been too lucky in love though," she said, raising the bridge of her nose. "I used to like someone in college, but things never worked out there because of some problems in his family. Back then, I accepted that fate and started taking the arranged marriage proposals seriously. Hey dear, your wedding was arranged or love?" she asked me.

"What...mine?" I stammered, partly because I wasn't expecting that question and partly because I didn't know the answer myself.

Yes, I did know Siddharth since my childhood days and we were friends before our wedding; and yes, he did approach me privately before anyone else in the family spoke about us getting married. But then, technically there was never a love phase back then. How about now? I asked myself. Is there any love between us now? Am I not able to accept my life the way it is because we don't have any love between us at all? I was lost in my thoughts.

"Arranged with someone that I was familiar with, from before," I said in that confused state of mind.

"Best," she said. "Well, so, though it was difficult for me to consider absolutely unknown men for marriage, I still continued to look for proposals, till I found one which looked like someone that I thought I could get settled with. He was a Gurugram-based software engineer. I had met him twice before the wedding got finalised. The first time that we met was with the family at a restaurant in Allahabad itself. We took some time to speak to each other alone, and though our families appeared all right and were ready to get us married, we requested them to give us a little more time. The second time we met in Delhi; I had gone there to meet a friend and took that opportunity to see him again. Our family had told them all about my health and they appeared to have no problem with it. The guy, well his name was Pradeep," she took a pause, "he was also very positive with everything that I had told him about my health."

As Seema continued to narrate to me about this phase of her life, I could see her tone changing and her voice wavering.

"It was a very positive thing for me, Tanya, because somewhere in my heart I always knew that I will have to face many rejections because of my health, and I even did. Though they were not straightforward rejections, but the changed expressions and interest as soon as we told a family about my health history said it all. Thus, considering this attitude of theirs, the family and the boy overall, there was a mutual yes for the wedding and things were finalised," she stayed quiet for a while. I got up and gave her some water.

"Tea again?" I asked.

"No," she said and continued again. "There was a small ceremony at my house first to announce things in our community. In that, we exchanged a few gifts, called a handful of known people and announced the wedding dates. From then on, Tanya, things started changing. Their family members started sounding a little more arrogant and Pradeep started behaving, or I am not sure if he really got, busier. But then, a wedding does that to most people I guess, so it didn't come across as a big change or something that struck a chord in us. There were subtle confusions that occurred on the wedding day as well, but overall the rituals went fine and uneventful." She was quiet for a good five minutes after this.

"The first night that I spent with Pradeep shook me from inside. There was no conversation made, no questions asked and no time wasted, he came inside our room and asked me to strip my clothes straightaway. That night, not only I got naked, but I also felt naked in front of him. He came upon me like an animal and naïve that I was, all that I was wondering was whether this is what every woman faces. The next day, I got up in a weird state of mind, but then he was better during the day. He spoke to me about the food he likes, told me about his regular time to return from work and added some commentary on the Delhi weather as well. I wasn't too happy to talk to him, but yes, I was certainly a bit relieved. I told myself that I should stop over-thinking about the previous night and thought that probably boys do behave the way he did after a certain age because their needs are different.

One day, when he was getting ready for office, I told him that I wanted to find some work. Since I am a fashion designer, the opportunities will be immense in this city I had told him. That statement didn't appear to go too well with him, but he anyhow agreed to take me to a famous boutique where he said I can talk about my

49

work opportunities. That boutique itself decided to hire me for a short term project where they needed some fresh designs. The next day, which was my first day at work, I got up early, prepared our meal and got ready to go to the boutique. I wore a long flowing t-shirt and a casual pair of jeans. Something like this," she showed me a picture on her phone.

No wonder, as a designer she would have had multiple pictures for all kinds of dresses, I thought.

"Pradeep gave me a very intense look, he looked at me from top to bottom and said, *what the hell are you wearing heroine, are you out of your mind!* For a moment I got conscious because I thought maybe my t-shirt is torn from somewhere or my jeans have some problems. I had a quick look at myself in the mirror and asked him what was wrong.

What's wrong! He said staring into my eye. *You are a married lady, who do you want to seduce with these kinds of clothes now? Wear some decent salwar kameez. These curves, madam, he came near, held my waist and said, are my property. I don't want others to have a look at them.* He was rude, but I did change into a salwar kameez instead of asking him anything. Probably because I used to get too bored sitting at home the entire day and I badly wanted to work.

"After this episode, I worked peacefully for a week, but on the eighth exact day, he barged into my office during lunch hour. The moment he entered, I was discussing something with a male colleague in my office, seeing which he got furious. He didn't say anything in front of my colleagues or in the boutique. He just took me out of there, shouted at me as usual, shamed me and never let me work again." She had a weird smile on her face.

I think I was now beginning to know that smile of hers as the one which people learn to wear in order to hide their true emotions.

"How could you not know his true character even then, Seema? This behaviour is intolerable!" I was angry.

"I had tried hinting about it to my mother, dear, but she said that males could sometimes be possessive. She suggested me to cook more cuisines for him in order to get closer to him," she laughed.

"What about your in-laws? They never visited you all this while?" I was curious.

"In-laws? They visited us once in this duration. It was during Diwali time that year, some of his extended family members had come home too. Pradeep was very well-behaved in front of his family and I too had tried to be a good *bahu* as instructed by my mother. You won't believe, Tanya, in order to be good to his family I gave some extra attention to his younger cousin, who was in the eighth standard and Pradeep had a problem with that too. That night, he shamed me for getting close to that twelve-year-old!"

"Eeeeeeeks!" I couldn't control myself from giving that reaction. "How could you not shout about it and tell it to his parents, to your friends, to your family, to just anybody?" I was loud.

"Dear, when I never got any supportive response from my mother herself then whom else could I have trusted. I didn't want to make a mockery out of my life. I knew my shortcomings, I knew my health, I didn't want to be a burden for my parents," she spoke casually, while I was still burning in rage.

"Then how did you land up here for an abortion? I am assuming that you are separated now?" I asked.

"Yes, the divorce has been filed but things are still under process," she said and I thanked God for that.

"Well, this happened because of an intolerable incident," she said. "That same night, he asked me to strip off my clothes as usual. But I quietly told him that I was having my monthly periods. He said it didn't matter and forced me further. Despite my requesting and pleading him, he satisfied his burning desire through my bleeding canal. I cried in pain that day and the next day I had to be admitted to the hospital because my pain just didn't stop. The entire family came to know about my situation and my father stood up for me and immediately took me back to Allahabad. On further investigations here, I was told that I was pregnant."

"Hey, but you had your periods you said, how could you be pregnant?" I was confused.

"Yes, I was experiencing bleeding, which made me think that I was having my periods, but the doctors said that I was already one month pregnant. What I experienced they said is called implantation bleeding, which is minor and can be experienced by pregnant women," she explained. "We thus aborted the child and filed for a divorce."

"And I am glad for both," was my reaction.

I continued meeting Seema for quite some time after this. I am happy that I was able to motivate her to talk about her experiences and the harsh realities that women have to face at a social gathering of her community later that month. I told her that the best she could do with her experience was to save other women and to strengthen other women who may be suffering quietly like her. That evening while I sat in the gathering where Seema spoke, I could see a confident young girl who suffered, cried, laughed and finally stood up through all her problems. How many centuries would it take I wondered, to make all the other Seema's hidden in many other portions of the country stand up for their own selves? Later that day, while Siddharth and I sat in our bedroom late at night, I asked him, "What is the importance of sex in marriage? Is it something that determines everything else?"

"Of course not!" he said. "But the problem with most men is that they grow up learning about it and fantasising it right since their adolescence. Tanya, anything is always more exciting in fantasies. Unable to match the real-life scenarios with their imaginations, men start both forcing it upon their partners and giving it more importance than they should. It is something which should never form the base of any relation, it is something that should rather coexist with other essential aspects of a relation," he said and got back to reading some book that he was reading then.

Siddharth had never forced me to get physical with him, not even if I denied it for months together. After having known Seema's story, a part of the rebel in me had mellowed down; the man beside me was certainly a nice man. But, how did it matter? I contradicted my own thoughts, because I was still compromising in so many other ways. Even after Sid slept, I was awake till late at night that day, thinking whether we had any love between us.

CHAPTER 6

SWAPNA

I finally spotted the yellow and white house that Swapna had told me about over the phone, **Reddy's** is what was written on the metallic board that hung outside it.

Since I had stayed in Hyderabad city for two good years before I got married, I had a decent idea about the roads and means of transport in the city. It was back then when I had made very good friends with Swapna, who was my colleague in the tech company where I was working then. Immediately after getting down at the airport, I had booked a cab for Swapna's house because as per my knowledge the airport Pushpak bus service didn't go till the Banjara Hills area, and that was where her house was.

"Hey!" A pregnant Swapna opened the door, gave me a warm hug and welcomed me to her house. "I hope you didn't have much problem in locating my house," she said.

"Hey, not at all; and look at you, you're glowing in joy!" I remarked.

"Nothing, madam, look at me as a whole also. One big fat whale I have become," she laughed as she ushered me in the house and made me sit in the living room.

What had taken me to Hyderabad was a short creative project. I was writing dialogues for a play and the director required me to stay in the city till the project got over. Since I didn't have a full-time job, I used to keep myself engaged by taking up such small creative projects. Unfortunately, I didn't have too many of them, but yes these were the ones that kept me surviving. Swapna had insisted that I should stay with her, but considering the privacy I need while I am writing, I had rather booked a serviced apartment for myself.

"Come two days prior to joining work, stay with me for two days at least," she had requested and thus I had landed at her place to see her.

Her house was simple yet huge. The living room area where I was seated then had the basic old-style sofas and a small round table which was kept in the centre. The place smelled of jasmine flowers, which I assumed were offered to the Gods who had a dedicated room, which I could see was located right adjacent to the open kitchen where Swapna was preparing some tea for me. She was in the eighth month of her pregnancy and unlike me, who had left all tech work after I got married, she was still continuing to work with the same company. Though she was draped in a loose flowing dress, I could still make out her prominent belly and the weight she had put on overall. Unlike the big fat whale that she addressed herself as, she looked mature and beautiful.

"How has pregnancy been for you till now, Swapna? I always imagine what it feels like to bear a child," I started my conversation with her.

"Don't ask! There are some things that I can describe and some things that I guess I can't," she said. "When we started planning for pregnancy, both me and Prithvi, my husband, thought it would be a cake-walk to conceive a child. But, Tanya, it was a task. We had to try for more than six months, imagine. We had almost given up and planned on consulting the gynaecologist but then that month, I luckily conceived. I was both relieved and happy with that," she held my hand and laughed.

"You won't believe the extent to which I am pampered nowadays. It's a great feeling that way. Do you remember our boss Satheesh, who used to get cranky and picky at everything? Imagine even he behaves very sweetly with me," she laughed.

"He is still there! Thank god I left the company," I said and we laughed more together.

"Even the company, in general, had no issues with the casual leaves which I took in plenty every now and then," she was excited while she narrated that.

"But as of now, you are on maternity leave right?" I asked her.

"Yes, yes, so it began just yesterday for me. Now that I have entered the eighth month, my family members didn't want me to attend office. Though I was okay only, I could have easily attended the office till the last day I feel."

What she said sounded great to me, because from many other narratives that I had heard from other women about their pregnancy, I used to feel that I would be confined to a corner of my home for that entire nine-month duration. It depends on person to person I thought.

"How about the health in general, how has that aspect been?" I probed further.

"Yes, so now you are talking." She stretched herself on the sofa and said, "Health, in general, hasn't been as perfect as it is when you are not bearing a life inside you. For the first trimester, which is the initial three months of pregnancy, I used to feel unusually weak for no reason. There were days when I just didn't feel like getting up from my bed at all, and if I did, it was only to vomit. But luckily, Tanya, since I was working, such days were rare and thus I could easily overcome that period. The other problem was sleeping, so it took me a while to get used to sleeping with this bump. For the initial few months, I used to get too conscious to even sleep, because I was scared of putting extra pressure over my stomach. You know right, I sleep over my tummy," she said like a true friend and I nodded a yes. "Then once I got adjusted to it, the bump size increased and now my problems were different! So all in all, Tanya, I am now an insomniac," she laughed loudly and so did I.

"So you have been here in Hyderabad itself since the start of it."

"Oh yes," she said. "Actually, initially I had told Prithvi that I want to shift to Anantpur, my mother's place, but my in-laws were little reluctant about it. Then even my mother suggested me to continue my work and now I am happy I did. They do visit me very often, stay with us and go, so it's okay. But yes, here, instead of work I have double work because till today I am cooking for everyone in the house," she sighed.

"But you said even your mother-in-law is here, right?"

"Yes, she is, but she also works in a firm. She says she cooked throughout her pregnancy, so I can't say no to cooking, you see. But it's okay, at least I like my own cooked food better than hers."

I was extremely glad to see Swapna's attitude. A happy-go-lucky girl who had beautifully adapted to everything that came her way. But the set of things she told me next were things that I hope she hadn't adapted to.

"I will show you your room," she took me upstairs and opened one of the rooms for me.

"Hey, pretty house! And it's very spacious," I said, looking around before I entered my room.

"My father's choice is like that only, madam," she said. "He has got us the best out of the lot that was available in Banjara Hills. The area was a restriction because my father-in-law said they wanted something in this portion of the city only, my husband's workplace is also nearby. Else, we would have looked for more options in the popular gated communities across the city. The only thing that's a little troublesome for me here is that this is an independent house," she was saying when I interrupted her.

"One second Swapna, your father got you the place means?" I asked.

"Means it was a part of the things he gave me for my wedding. Even you have it no, this give and take thing?" she said casually.

"Dowry is what I normally name the give and take thing, lady!" I said it little lightly because I didn't want to take things on the serious turn for the eight-month-old pregnant, happy friend of mine.

"No, not dowry," she started casually again. "Whatever dad has given me is for our security, for my security. See, now I am only staying in this house, had it not been for this, they were staying in a rental place. Dowry is what they forcefully demand. Here it's like the parents mutually discuss everything prior to the wedding and what my parents have done is ultimately for me only," she explained.

"Okay. Great, what else did you receive from your father in the form of security for yourself?" I asked her.

"Actually, mostly, it's all in the form of gold. I have some crores worth of gold, some of which I have safely put in the locker and the rest which I can use is with me at home. He has also given me a Grand i10 separately, we use it commonly but if I need it, it's reserved for me."

"That's about all?" I was sarcastic, but Swapna didn't realise it and added more to her speech.

"We are thinking we may put up a small business, mostly food-related, in the days to come. See, now I will have a kid and I can't plan to work in this company forever. Once we finally decide to put the business up, my father said he would help us in starting it."

The human mind is such a weird organ, I thought. It has the capability of justifying anything that it feels is right. It is probably a result of the justifications that we give ourselves and the manipulative games that we play on others, that so many such obsolete things are still prevalent in our society. Naming dowry as security won't make a poor father spend lesser on his daughter's wedding, I thought. But, as I mentioned earlier, I put my logic and conflicts aside because, at that moment, a happy Swapna was more important for me. Later that day, I spent time with other members of her family after they came back home from their respective workplaces. I was warmly welcomed by each one of them. The next day, I left for my serviced apartment and promised Swapna and her family to keep visiting as long as I was in the city.

***

"No, madam, you have written it well but it is not conveying the exact meaning as I want," said the director of the play to me during one of our sessions.

It was tedious and many a time a herculean task to get inside his head; to think exactly how he was thinking and write it likewise. It was almost ten in the night and the mild cold was now beginning to hit me. If you have been to Hyderabad in winter times, you would know that though you step out of your houses in light t-shirts or kurtas during the day, you start feeling the need for a shawl or a jacket by the end of the day. Since we were roaming on the porch, I was feeling the need for a shawl more. To my rescue, I saw the sound engineer of the play approaching us from a distance.

"I will rewrite these by today itself, sir, I assure you we will be able to finish shooting this scene tomorrow," I was saying, by when he reached.

"Sir, I think Tanya should leave, a lot of ruckus is expected in the city. For her safety, I will drop her back," he said.

"What happened?" the director asked.

"Sir, a brutal rape has been reported somewhere near Shadnagar area. Things are still not clear, but we have overheard about this from our media friends."

"Dreadful!" he said and immediately asked me to go back.

Next morning and for the next few days, the entire country mourned with Hyderabad. A twenty-six-year-old veterinary doctor was brutally raped and burnt dead by four men, the news said. I got endless calls from my family to ask about my safety; my mother asked me to leave the project and return back to Allahabad. But will I be safe there, I asked her. Will I be safe anywhere? It was very difficult for me to work for the next few days because anger had taken over creativity. Though a little reluctantly, I continued working on the project in an attempt to finish it. While on my way to the theatre where the practice sessions of the play were held then, I could see the roads crowded with different forms of protests every now and then. While the common man got together with candles and mourned and marched for the deceased, groups which supported the opposition party then were seen protesting and demanding justice from the government. While this ongoing tragedy took new turns every day, I took a new scene every day with an aim to finish the dialogues and could finally say a closure to my work within the next eight days.

I had booked my flight for a day later so that I could dedicate the next day buying some south Indian spices and saris from Hyderabad. But the next morning, I got up with multiple messages on my WhatsApp. There were forwarded posts from some friends and on some groups which said that the four accused in the doctor's rape case were shot dead by the police. I could barely imbibe that news and before I could even think about what I had just read, I opened a message from Swapna's husband which read as,

We are blessed to have a baby girl! Both mother and child are doing fine.

That news overlapped the bigger news which had shaken the country once again, and I got ready at once to go and meet my dear friend and her family. Swapna had delivered her child in one of the poshest hospitals in the city. They did have many branches but the one where she delivered was in the Banjara Hills area near her house. The room where she was admitted had a private balcony, a bathroom, an extra bed, a cute cradle and a very beautiful overall décor. A happy but exhausted Swapna lay peacefully on her bed, while her husband stood by her side holding their beautiful daughter wrapped in a pink and white blanket.

"Awe ... She is adorable, can I take her picture?" I asked her.

"Yes, why not," Swapna smiled. "She has already posed for so many before."

I gifted her with a small basket of baby goodies which I had picked up from a store on my way and took her leave. While I was getting out of the hospital, I saw her father involved in an argument with the receptionist.

"How can the hospital add that many charges at the last moment? Do you even know how much eighty thousand is?" her father was saying.

The next moment I spotted her mother, who was sitting in the reception lobby with a worried expression.

"Greetings Aunty, is all good?" I approached her.

She looked up in haste, "Oh, you are Swapna's friend right? How are you? She was just telling you are in the city."

"Yes, Aunty, I am fine and I met her. Her daughter is adorable, just like her," I smiled. "I was going out but I stopped by because I saw uncle at the reception. Do you need any help? Should I intervene? Or should I call Prithvi?" I asked.

"No, no," she held my hand. "Your uncle will sort it. This hospital is too expensive, we had set a deal at two lakh rupees actually, but they are adding some huge additional fee at the last moment that is why he is talking to them. He did not expect that much at the end and is not carrying that money. His card is also blocked, so he will have to make arrangements from Anantpur now, talk to the bank and all that."

"But Aunty, Prithvi is just upstairs. I will go tell him to pay," I almost got up.

"No," she pulled my hand. "In our side, it is considered auspicious to bear the charges for daughter's first pregnancy, that's why I can't ask them," she said.

I sat down.

"The girl's in-laws decide whichever place is good in the city and we as parents arrange things accordingly. For me also my parents had only borne the cost of it, but in those times it was not so expensive," she laughed.

"I will take your leave, Aunty," I said, "and congratulations once again for a beautiful granddaughter."

The next day as I waited at the boarding gate of my flight, I looked at Swapna's daughter's picture. Her eyes were closed and unaware of all the drama that we adults were entangled in, she slept peacefully.

"Raise your voice loud when you grow up, my darling, and tell your father that it's you who would rather make his old age secure. Tell him that he doesn't need to struggle in his retirement days to pay for your gold, for your house and for your health. Know that the wrongs and the bad won't always look wrong and bad, it is you who will have to use your wit to understand what's wrong and what's bad," I murmured to her picture.

In a world that was becoming unsafe for women every day, I prayed for her safety and finally recalled and read the Hyderabad police encounter news in detail. After which I opened my twitter account and typed,

I salute the Hyderabad police for their bold move and I am glad that in the recent rape and murder case things took a faster track than usual. But no matter how great it sounds, this isn't justice delivered. For such crimes, we now need a firm law from the judiciary instead of more such heroic attempts!

CHAPTER 7

NIHARIKA

The rape tragedy in Hyderabad had disturbed me a lot. In a continuation with the series of it, there was yet another tragedy in Unnao city that made news in the upcoming days. My Instagram used to be full of women empowerment posts; my WhatsApp was usually flooded with messages on women's safety and defence. Different talk shows on both the television and the radio discussed the possible solutions to raise safety amongst women. The entire country seemed to be bothered about women, and both the genders seemed to have been affected and moved by the incidences then. But, unfortunately, women were still unsafe!

"It bothers me, Siddharth, and I am surprised to see so many of them survive through such brutal incidences. What are they made of? How do they overcome this?" I looked at him and asked.

"I can't make up an answer for it, and I can't answer that through my philosophy as well. Why don't you meet one of them and ask?" he suggested.

I started my research about women and the brutality they face every year. Not only were they victims of rape from men who wanted to fulfil their sexual desires, but also, they were sufferers of their rage which many of them had faced in the form of acid attacks. I remembered having gotten angry at Siddharth once for spilling a soft drink on me accidentally at a party.

"Where is your orientation, Doc?" I had said in front of a friend of ours, "Is this how you perform your surgeries as well? By spilling medicines on open cuts."

Siddharth had chosen to remain quiet then but had later mentioned that I should try and control my words. Those were the days immediately after our wedding; days when I used to remain unusually frustrated thinking that I had been trapped in a life full of compromises. I was ashamed thinking about my behaviour back then, but as they say, words once said and an arrow once shot cannot be taken back. Thus I had decided to be more aware while speaking anything from then on. I got lost in that past and suddenly shivered to imagine what it would be like to face a forceful acid attack and the life that follows it.

I remembered having met a girl who was working as a typist in a small shop where I had gone to get a print-out once. She had helped me connect my pen drive to the system where she was typing then, after which she had quietly handed over the print to me. She was wearing dark glasses over her eyes and her face was partially covered with a veil that she had tightly draped over her head. I had looked at her for more than a moment because I had noticed that her skin looked different from most of us.

"A boy had thrown acid over her face some years back," the owner of the shop told me in a low voice when I was paying for my prints. He had probably noticed me looking at her in a strange way. Naïve that I was back then, I had barely gone into the depth of it. This again was immediately after my wedding when I was settling my documents for a new bank account in the city. It was almost three years since then and I wasn't sure if I would find her in the same shop, but I took my chance.

Two random men stood on the other side of the counter in that shop.

"I was actually looking for..." I said looking around when one of them, who appeared more impatient, started dealing with another customer who had come and stood beside me.

As I stood there wondering what to ask, a man who was seated in a corner stood up and came to me.

"Madam, do you want to get a Xerox done?" he asked.

He looked like the owner of the shop, though as far as my remembrance went, he had no resemblance with the man that I had met previously at the same shop. But anyway, he looked more mature than the sales boys so I took him aside and asked,

"Actually I had come here long back. A girl used to work here back then."

I was playing with my words when he said, "Niharika?"

I looked at him in confusion. I had no idea what her name was.

"The girl on whom acid had been thrown right?" he said, spitting his pan.

Wow, he had come straight on point.

"Yes," I said hesitantly.

"She was the only female staff that has ever worked here, that too for just two months."

"Oh, okay. I am sorry to have bothered you. I actually wanted to speak to her and was wondering if she was still here. Thanks anyway," I said with a gesture to leave.

"Wait," he stopped me. "She goes to that computer training institute," he pointed out to a distant building on the opposite side of the road. "If you really want to meet her, then try talking to someone there," he suggested.

"Thank you so much. That was a great help," I said and left the place.

I went to that training centre next.

"Yes, ma'am?" the receptionist interrupted me from entering further in.

"I am looking for Miss Niharika. I am not known to her but I need to speak to her for something personal," I gave her my card.

While the receptionist was reading my details, someone interrupted from behind.

"Do I know you?" a female voice asked.

I turned back and there she was in front of my eyes.

"Niharika?" I asked and she nodded a yes.

"No, you don't. Can we talk?" I said and we sat on the chairs laid in the waiting area of the reception.

I introduced myself to her, gave her a brief about myself, my book and about how I managed to reach her.

"I understand your concern, but..." she paused, "I have never discussed it with anyone before."

I chose to remain quiet; I didn't want to market myself.

She asked me a few things about myself, my husband, my family, my education and so on and so forth. I answered her about everything very patiently.

"Not that I am mistrusting you, but can you please give me some time? I will get back to you with an answer," she said.

"Of course," I smiled, "please take all your time," I said, gave her my card and left the centre.

I didn't hear from her for almost a week. I had decided not to approach her again because I didn't want to force anyone to open up; it was her wish after all. But just when I had given up on expecting a call from her, she called.

"Hello, Tanya *didi*," she said over the phone. "Can you come to my centre today?"

I was extremely happy to have heard from her because her call was proof that she could trust me.

"Should we go and sit in some quiet place?" she asked.

"Sure," I said and we went to an open park in the city.

It was the month of December and the afternoon sun in the park was all that we needed. The grass that we were walking on was mildly wet; it was the dew, I guess. While we took the first two rounds of the park we walked in utter silence, after which she spoke herself.

"I am twenty-four now, I was eighteen then. I belong to a basic lower middle class family, but my parents gave my education equal priority as my younger brother. They did the best they could to get me educated in an English medium school in the city. After schooling, I had gotten myself enrolled in the B.Com. course in Lucknow city. It was the first time that I was staying away from my house but, *didi,* trust me, I didn't forget my rules and my values," she explained.

I didn't know why she was bringing her values in between, but I waited to hear further.

"I used to be back to my paying guest accommodation on time, cook by myself and go out on rare occasions with friends. Mine was an only girls college and it was usually my female friends from college that I went out with. Some of them did have male friends who used to occasionally show up with them. Once during a birthday party of one such female friend of mine, she invited a gang of her male friends from school. We all had met for lunch in a restaurant, after which we parted our ways. The next day, my friend mentioned to me about a boy Sameer who had come to attend the lunch party; she said he had fallen in love with me at first sight. They all started teasing me about him and suggested that I should plan to meet him or watch a movie with him on some occasion. But, *didi,*" she held my hand, "I knew how hard my father was working to pay my fees and I told them I didn't want to involve in any such thing. I swear on my mother, *didi,* I said that and I was not interested in getting involved at all."

With the way she was explaining things to me, I assumed that maybe people have told her time and again that it was she who was at fault in that entire incidence, but anyway I kept hearing her patiently.

"My friend said she conveyed about my disinterest to Sameer, but I guess he wasn't able to digest that rejection. He once came and stood beneath my accommodation in the morning while I was leaving for college and offered me a lift on his bike. I got scared to see him there and started walking away in haste. He followed me and tried speaking to me, and when I didn't respond, he publicly shouted, 'What for are you carrying that attitude, madam? Do you think you are pretty? One day you will hate to even look at yourself!' I was scared and I told my friend about it. I also requested her to convey him not to bother me again. Even she was surprised by his attitude but she asked me to take it lightly and said she would speak to him for sure.

For the next few days, things were normal and I didn't have any botheration at all. In fact, two months passed and I went home for Diwali. I had forgotten about Sameer's episode and thus never mentioned it to my parents. I didn't want to bother them with it. As my friend had suggested, I took it lightly.

After I returned back to Lucknow, one day while I was returning back from my college in an auto, a sudden splash came over me. A splash that had made my vision hazy. I didn't know what that feeling was? In an attempt to see what had just happened, I rubbed my eyes to remove that liquid, but unfortunately, I wasn't able to see anything clearly even after that. In the haze that I had in front of my eyes, I could partially see and feel my hair burning off. All of a sudden, the *dupatta* that I was wearing over my dress then stuck over my body. I felt a sudden and strong burning pain and shouted loudly. The auto that I was in was passing from near a hospital in the city centre and the driver was kind enough to take me to the hospital. I don't know the series of events that followed for the next couple of hours because my pain had blanked me out completely. What was even more disturbing to me at that point was that I was not able to see a single thing around.

After some time on the same day, I could hear some familiar voices around me, my friends and then my parents. The first thing that I heard from my mother was her cry. I could feel that they were all seeing something terrible in me, something that shook them, because shocking reactions and cries around were unstoppable till the night. My mother held my hands and I told her that I would be all right. I told her that it was a matter of just one or two months and things would be good, but *didi,* it was only after two months passed by that I realised that I was victimised and deformed forever."

While Niharika continued to narrate her story to me, I continued to admire the courage with which she spoke. I continued to notice that unlike the small things that made my eyes well up, she stood there with me without a single hitch in her voice. We then sat on the pavement in some tree shade and she continued again.

"I underwent eighteen surgeries to look finally the way I look now. I never saw my face immediately after the attack because I had turned blind but all that I felt over my face was bone and flesh. I displayed a lot of courage until I had hope in me, but once I realised that I won't be the same again, fear overtook all my emotions. In the closed chambers of the hospital, I used to get nightmares and cold shivers. I used to get flashes of the attack and used to hide under the bed or in my quilt to feel better. I had to be shifted to a bigger hospital to get the skin grafts over my face done. They took skin from my thigh, my back and the lower portion of my legs and grafted it in patches that you can see all over my face now," she said, looking at me. "Along with these surgeries, I also had regular sessions with a psychiatrist who made me much stronger and reduced my nightmares. I was still blind but; I felt paralysed without vision. We consulted some doctors and spoke to them about the possibilities of a cornea transplant to get back my vision. But not one or two, more than ten doctors said no for the procedure. I was in despair but my mother stood by me as strongly as she could. She hadn't been working till then but in an attempt to improve the financial status of my family, she started teaching in a primary school. She said if her eyes could get back my lost vision, she was ready to go blind for me. Mothers are strange, right *didi*?" She was quiet.

"We finally found a ray of hope in a renowned hospital in Chennai, where they said they were ready to work on my vision. The eyes, however, they said may not look the same as they do in most other people. I would be happy with the vision I had told them and they started with their procedures. I stayed in Chennai for one long year until they worked on my eyes. Multiple skin grafts were again taken from various portions of my body, including the inside of my mouth. They had torn apart the skin from my gums as well. After a long wait when they finally uncovered my eyes, I slowly got adapted to seeing the world the way it was, but the biggest challenge was lying just ahead of me. That challenge was to finally see my transformed self after two long years. My parents were scared as to how I will react and so they didn't allow me to look at myself immediately. They first got me used to my new vision and took me back home; there as well they removed all mirrors from the house to first get me back to a stable state of mind. But I happened to see myself accidentally over my phone's screen one day and my scream I am sure must have been heard till my neighbourhood that day."

I remembered how upset I was one day when I had gotten three new pimples on my forehead just on the day of some event. I was sure that no matter how hard I tried, I would just fail to empathise with how Niharika would have felt on seeing herself.

"From that day onwards, I was shattered. I didn't want to face the world; I didn't want to scare them rather. One afternoon while I was alone in the house, I decided to end my life. I tied a rope around the fan and stood up on a chair to hang myself from it. The moment I held the rope to place it around my neck, multiple thoughts crowded in my mind. I looked around the house, my parents had put it on stake just to pay the bills for my surgeries, I looked at my books, despite paying my fees with great difficulty my parents had considered me an equal and proudly invested on my education. I looked at myself, despite the society raising thousands of fingers on me unaware of my sufferings, my parents had killed all their pride and were still there by my side. *What a fool you are, to even think of ending your life*, I had told myself that day. From that day onwards, I never looked back, *didi,* and I have been fighting to do whatever I can for myself. I didn't have the strength to go back to college. Thus, I started doing multiple other things. You must have seen me in that printer shop in the duration immediately after that. I realised I had to acquire more skills to earn more. Thus I have enrolled myself in multiple courses since then."

"What about that boy, Niharika?" I finally broke my silence.

"Sameer?" she asked. "No one has any evidence about who had done it," she took a pause. "Since I was blinded, I wasn't able to look up at all. The auto driver had decided to take me to the hospital first instead of chasing him, and by the time people on the road realised what had happened with me inside the auto, the two boys on the bike had disappeared, they say. To be honest, even I can't ascertain that it was him, but with what he had told me that day when he chased me, and with the rage that he had on me, I can't think of anyone else who could have done this."

This time I saw a quiet tear roll down her cheeks.

I hugged her and she rested her head over my shoulder.

"He had said that one day I would hate to even look at myself in the mirror and I thought I would prove him wrong. He would have thrown that acid on my face thinking that he would spoil my life, but I will make it bigger and better." She held me tight and so did I.

"You are women of valour and courage, my beautiful Niharika. You are a woman who has risen out of the ashes like a phoenix and who is, I am sure, unstoppable now and can do anything that she wants." I planted a kiss on her forehead.

I asked her the details of the training session that was she attending then, and also asked her about her interests. I guided her to apply to an institute in Pune, where she could get trained further in her field of interest. I mentioned to her about a unique and beautiful café in Lucknow and Agra cities of Uttar Pradesh, which was run by acid attack victims. Sheroes, as it was rightly named, was a one of its kind place where I had once attended an open mike session. She was thrilled to hear about it and said she would visit there someday soon. Niharika and I exchanged our numbers and promised to stay in touch with each other.

How difficult would it have been for Niharika, I thought, to face a world that revolves around a woman's looks? No matter how much the society says that it doesn't bother about looks, it still does. The list of beauty pageant competitions across the world are more than ever before. They say that they focus on the holistic aspects of a woman's personality but why do we then have those thin, tall women with beaming and flawless skin wearing the most perfect dresses on those ramps? Why do we then have those makeup products which sponsor those events and those beauticians who paint the pageants for it? If we didn't bother about looks at all, then why wouldn't we dare to conduct such events in one's natural skin and hair? Keeping aside the show world, even in our real everyday world a matrimonial advertisement for a woman still reads *tall, fair and attractive* very commonly. There are so many women, I thought, who still undergo a tedious ceremony after their wedding where other women from across the city or village where they get married, come, lift their veil and look at them one by one. And forget about the real world, even the virtual world of social media and cell phones have apps with ever-rising filter options to post the most perfect pictures. If all this that still prevails around us, doesn't shout that it's all about looks then what else will? I was proud that Niharika had learned to fight in this difficult world of ours. She had literally risen up from her ashes; she was someone that the entire world could look up to and could learn from. How easily I get disheartened on facing the smallest of issues, I thought; she was someone that I could learn so much from. I felt terrible thinking about the man who would have done such a thing without knowing the consequences that she would have to face for it for the rest of her life. I felt even worse thinking how such men who commit such heinous crimes escape so easily.

"Don't we need to act upon the basics in our country first? Don't we need safety, education and food for all before we talk about more metro rails, more satellites and more statues?" I expressed my anger to Siddharth after returning home.

"I won't make any comment on that, Tanya," he said, "but I can assure you that we definitely need more people like you and me, who are educated and aware to come out and do their bit for the society and for the people around them to gradually bring bigger and more permanent changes in the country!"

CHAPTER 8

CHANDRAMMA

It was 10am already, but I was still lazing in my bed. It was one of those days when I just didn't feel like getting up. Siddharth had left for the hospital at eight in the morning; I had served him tea and breakfast and slept again. Sunita was on leave so I didn't have any further motivation to get up.

"Why do I have to make my own breakfast?" I frowned and said to myself.

It is so nice at my mother's place, I thought, where no matter when I get up there is always some food ready. With great motivation, I left my bed, kneaded some flour and made pooris for myself. I felt unusually dull without any reason. I didn't feel like writing anything at all, I just stared into some blank space thinking about nothing.

After a while of feeling that way, I realised that it might be because I was in my premenstrual time. Premenstrual syndrome, which I am sure had severe mood impact on me, affected many other women I knew as well. Lethargy, irritability, dullness and minor aches are common symptoms which a woman faces because of the hormonal alterations that she undergoes a few days before her periods. While the lucky ones are understood by their husbands for behaving unusually in this duration, the less fortunate ones have a more difficult time. While I sat doing nothing my phone buzzed, it was Siddharth as usual. "Hey Tanya, I just got a message. There is a small get together in my alumni medical college this weekend. Would you like to accompany me?"

"Hey, sure, why not?" I said, "You know I love meeting new people."

***

Siddharth's alumni college was in the city of Lucknow. Built on what was once the outskirts of the city, it was now more or less a part of the city itself because of the rapid construction of buildings and markets around it. The moment we entered the campus, we experienced a temperature drop of around three to four degrees. Surrounded by a lot of greenery, it was a calm and peaceful place. The provision for our accommodation was made in the guest house of the campus. After having reached, we took a while to rest and unwind, after which the meetings and greetings started. The formal event was arranged by the institute during the lunch hours. Since we had reached much earlier to that, we strolled in the hall of the guest house to look around and meet people on a more casual note before the event began.

"Hey Tanya, let me introduce you to Meghna," Sid said. "She was my junior in college, got married early back then, had a child and is now back to specialising in this college as an ophthalmologist."

"Wow, great meeting you," I said. After which I was quietly overhearing their college time talks when a lady with a child joined us. She was Meghna's mother-in-law.

"*Amma*, how come you are here?" Meghna looked surprised.

"Yes, I came to pick Summi up from her art classes. They do it here only in this building," she pointed at her daughter and said.

"Oh! Yes. We have alumni meet right, so people who have come are staying here in this building. He is Siddharth sir, my senior from college, and his wife Tanya," she introduced us to her.

Her mother-in-law was very talkative, and while those two continued their discussion, she started speaking to me about my education etc.

"You have studied at Manipal! Wow," she was thrilled to hear that from me. "We belong to Mangalore; all of it is *Dakshin* Karnataka. What weather, what food!" she appeared lost.

"*Howdu* Aunty," I said, accidentally using one word in the Kannada language. This got her even more excited.

"Wow, you speak Kannada. Come home and have lunch with me. I have prepared some yummy chutney. You will remember your Manipal days, what will you do here anyway. Isn't it Summi, should we take Aunty home for food?" she asked her granddaughter.

"Come, Aunty," Summi pulled my hand.

Sid didn't say anything; he just raised his eyebrow slightly, which meant your wish.

The quarters where Meghna stayed with her family was a small two-room apartment. With Summi's toys scattered everywhere, her drawings scribbled on the walls, unwashed clothes piled up in one corner of the house and relatively bigger beds in smaller rooms, the place looked congested. I was made to sit in one of the rooms, while Aunty made the three-year-old Summi change her clothes and wash her hands. She then cut a bowl full of fruits for all of us and finally sat down.

"It's so cold here," she started, "gets very difficult for me sometimes. You know how the weather in our portion of the country is," she said, rubbing her foot with one hand and feeding Summi with the other.

"I understand, Aunty; it must be really difficult for you. How often do you travel back to Mangalore?" I asked her.

"I haven't travelled for more than six months now. Your uncle is also alone there. He manages things because of some of our relatives."

"Oh, that must be difficult too," I said.

"But what can be done? These two here, both my son and daughter-in-law are so busy. Now someone has to look after their home and family as well. I think women are far more privileged nowadays; they have better access to education and more acceptance of their careers in the society unlike in our times. I never got a chance to read that much. I was married before I knew what the outside world was like. I hadn't even met your uncle in person before getting married to him. The day I saw him for the first time was on the day of our wedding."

"What was your age then?" I asked.

"Oh, I was barely eighteen. Though my actual name is Chandramma, my in-laws used to call me Chandra out of love because I was a little girl for them. I had finished my twelfth standard of school, that's it. I wanted to study further but that was never an option for me or a choice that I could have made. I wanted to be a lawyer. I used to imagine myself like a confident woman in that black and white attire we see in courts. I mean I have mostly seen them on television like that, but yes, that's what I wanted to be," she sighed and laughed at the same time. "Times have changed, they have changed for good but they have changed! God knows how many more changes I will see till I am alive. Imagine what it will be like till my little baby gets married," she took Summi on her lap and said.

I looked outside the house and all I could see were cold and dry roads with similarly quiet apartments.

"Do you have other people around from Mangalore on this campus?" I asked.

"There are some young couples, but they are all doctors. They are all so busy, where they get time to visit or talk. Everyone rushes for their classes or work early in the morning and they are back only by night."

"And what do you do by the day when no one is around?" I asked again.

"I just cook, take her to two of her classes and talk over the phone. What else can I do here? We have a maid who comes to clean the house, but I don't understand her Hindi so I don't speak much to her as well."

I shouldn't have asked her that question I thought. I could imagine the level of loneliness and boredom that she would be facing on a daily basis, no wonder she was desperate to take me home and was talking so much. I could empathise with her more because I knew what it felt like to sit at home and do nothing. Ever since I had started writing, I was a bit relieved as otherwise it used to get very annoying for me.

"Back then when I had gotten married, Tanya," she continued, "though I had not been able to complete my education I had accepted that situation of mine wholeheartedly. I had been supportive of my husband in his business. He owned a small jewellery shop. I used to stay with my in-laws and his brother. Though I used to be at home for most of the day, it never pricked me that much because some or the other festival or ritual always kept us ladies busy. My father-in-law passed away at an early age and then the responsibility of the shop came entirely upon the two brothers. Though they tried their best to manage things together, there was always some or the other misunderstanding between them. They thus decided to open two separate shops in two different areas. After a few days, my brother-in-law shifted to another house as well. My mother-in-law was alive till my second son, Meghna's husband, was delivered. A few months later, she too passed away. In the years ahead, your uncle worked very hard to grow the shop and he even managed to do well with time. It was very taxing for me to bring up both these sons together," she appeared lost in her past.

"We educated them to the best of our capabilities, the elder one was in your Manipal College only for his Bachelor's in Technology," she pointed. "The younger one had a different interest altogether and moved out to Delhi to study medicine. A few years later, the elder son too flew to the US to pursue his Master's. Since then, Tanya, we never had our children back home. After we had two sons, we too had dreamt of a big happy family whom we imagined would stay together. But who says sons stay with you forever! Times have changed, my daughter, times have changed," she again looked at Summi and said.

"Women of my generation have spent most of our lives taking care of others. We have always been confined to our houses and that's what our world has been like. We were always married as caretakers of our husbands. We patiently built their families, compromised everything for our children. But even our children aren't with us anymore, we stay with them or they stay with us only till their kids are young, and the moment they grow up and start going to school, we are back to our pavilion. Your uncle spent a lot of his income to build such a big house, three floors we have," she stressed on three, "but it's all empty. The world has become smaller now; everyone flies off wherever they find an opportunity. Doesn't matter where your home is, doesn't matter where your roots are," she looked upset.

"My elder son had gone to the US for his Master's I told you, but now he is happily settled there with wife and kids. We don't travel there often, and then even his kids are grown up now," she laughed. "My other son, this one, he told me last month that he and Meghna are planning on joining their friend's hospital in Delhi after they complete their tenure here. Your uncle and I will stay alone in that big house doing what, we don't know! I don't know whether it's good or bad. But since these changes happened so rapidly in the past years, at least people of my age have faced some brunt of it," she was vocal in expressing her experiences.

My heart sank; all of a sudden, I remembered one of my maternal grandmothers whom I had met in Jaipur a few years back. I had stayed with her for two days because I had a small conference in the city and my parents didn't want me to take the risk of staying alone in a hotel. She had a stooped back; Kyphosis is what it is called in medical terminology. It was stooped to the extent that when I had first seen her, I thought she was sitting and only later I realised about her deformity. When I had entered further inside her house, she introduced me to her husband, my maternal grandfather, who was paralysed and lay in one of the rooms. To my surprise, it was just the two of them in their huge house. Granny had swiftly climbed up with her deformity to show me my room and then climbed back to give me some water and snacks upstairs in the room itself. *Be here and do your work, you will have all your privacy here,* she had told me. I was embarrassed. I didn't need any privacy. But the more I told her that I was all right and I didn't need anything, the more checks she had made on me throughout the day, this was a day prior to my conference day. Maybe she is used to people expecting privacy I had thought. I had chosen to spend most of my time downstairs in her room from the next day onwards and it was then that she had told me more and more things about herself. "My daughter stays in Melbourne with her family and my son is in the US," she had told me. "Our son calls us every weekend and makes sure to talk to us for long. He doesn't get much time to visit India, because besides work he also has his own business in Seattle. And look at us," she had smiled, "we can't afford to travel with these bodies."

Meghna's mother-in-law was right, I thought, at least we in our generation knew that our children won't be around and won't be ours after having finished their education. With the westernisation of culture and with the ever-growing technology, that's how the trend had become. But most people of her age would have silently suffered for sure.

"It's lunchtime, come we will eat," she told me and I had joined her in the kitchen for warming the food and serving it on plates.

She had cooked a very specific dish from the state of Karnataka called the *jawar roti*, along with some brinjal curry and tomato chutney. I remembered having it in my mess sometimes, but what she had cooked tasted entirely different from my mess food and had brought a big smile on my face. We had some lighter conversation after that and by the time I decided to leave, Meghna entered the house.

"You came early today?" her mother-in-law asked in excitement.

"No Ma, I will change and leave for the alumni function now. I got very late so couldn't go there for lunch. I have eaten something in the canteen. My Summi, my baby, how have you been?" she hugged her child and planted some kisses on her cheeks.

"I get to see her so rarely," she looked at me and said.

"I can imagine, I know how a doctor's schedule is like!" I told her.

"Did you guys have lunch?" she asked me.

"Yes, and I loved what aunty made," I had told her.

"She is such a great cook. In fact, she takes care of most of the things in the house in our absence. I am able to leave Summi and pursue my education and work, all because of her. I can't tell you how fortunate I am to have her around," she mentioned with tears that had welled up in her eyes.

"Hey, it's okay," I kept my hand on her shoulder. "Maybe the best you can do is spend some time with her as and when you can," I suggested, calming her down.

Meghna then gave me a brief on how she often gets guilty of missing out on the small and big moments of motherhood, and how she tries her best to maintain a balance between her duties and her daughter.

"Hey, if you are done talking to aunty then you can join me in the auditorium." Sid called me and said. "They are beginning to perform a skit followed by some musical sessions for us."

"Sure, I will be there," I told him.

As I exited out of the accommodation, I looked around at the other houses in that residential premise. I didn't know how many other such Meghna's and their mothers-in-law stayed in each one of those. While the two were completely supportive and loving towards each other, they were a trap in their own circumstances and had their individual battles to fight. But isn't the battle that we fight with our own selves the most difficult of them all! Like the one I fought with myself every day. The battle to know myself more, the battle to accept my husband more, and the battle to stay happier and more content with what I had.

CHAPTER 9

ROHINI

"*Didi*, someone has come to meet you," Sunita, my help, knocked the door of my room one morning.

"What is it, Sunita? Please ask them once. If it's a courier, please receive it," I told her.

I was busy writing and any external stimulus while I am writing comes across like a wave that interrupts my thoughts. I am sure that must be the case with other writers as well. Probably that's why we had or still have writers who choose to completely isolate themselves in the hills etc. while they are writing. The best that I do for isolation is putting my phone on aeroplane mode, because well, that is perhaps the hub of disturbance for most of us nowadays-our cell phones.

"*Didi*, someone has come from the Philips Company. It seems you had complained about the iron box," Sunita reappeared.

"Oh! Yes, yes. Remember the new steam iron box which I just bought," I looked at Sunita, "it has been giving me serious trouble," I said, kept my laptop and notebook aside, and went out of the room.

I was surprised to see a woman waiting at the door. I looked at Sunita to confirm if she had come from the Philips Company for repair. *It's funny how people like me who claim to have the most advanced kind of thoughts when it came to women's equality, still get surprised to see women in the kind of roles where they normally expect a man.* Sunita nodded yes and I ushered that lady inside the drawing room.

"Here," I gave her the iron box. "We just bought it last month and it just doesn't generate any steam. Forget that, at times it fails to just heat up as well."

"Can I get a small chair to keep this?" she asked.

I gave her one and she started working on it. While she was working, I hung around in the hall just outside the drawing room and kept checking on her every now and then. I asked Sunita to serve her with a glass of water and she appeared extremely overwhelmed with that small gesture. After she finished her job, she asked me to check it well and since it was working just all right, I signed on the company papers.

"Madam, there is a small column below where you can rate and review my service, it will be very helpful if you could please fill it," she requested.

"Yes, sure, why not," I said and rated her excellent. She appeared thrilled with it.

"I didn't ask your name?" I said.

"Rohini," she said.

"Well, Rohini, you are doing a great job. I have seen very few women who are service providers for electronic goods. For how long have you been into it?" I complimented her and asked her simultaneously.

"Thank you so much, madam. I am with this company for almost one year now," she smiled. "Well great, a year isn't bad! And previously some other electronic company?" I asked and got up to usher her till the door again.

"No, madam, I wasn't working in this field previously."

"Oh okay, then? You had some other interest apart from electronics, is it?" I casually asked.

"No, madam. It's better if I don't talk about it. And madam, many a time a girl doesn't get to choose what her interests are," she said.

"Yes, you are right. Most of the times, she doesn't get to choose what she likes. Like I can't choose to run from this house even if I don't like it," I laughed. "In fact, I am writing something about the multifaceted, complicated lives that women lead," I said, with an intention to make her more comfortable with me.

"Wow, you're a writer?" she asked.

"Yes, I am. I love listening to stories and bringing them to the fore. I believe stories have the power to bring about changes. I believe a happy story can motivate others, a challenging story can inspire others and ..." I was saying when she interrupted.

"And a sad story? I don't think it needs to be told; it can't be of any use because..."

"Well, a sad story and a difficult story is the most important type for the society, because out of all other stories that we keep hearing, that is the one which makes us learn the maximum out of all!" I said and smiled.

I could see some thrill in her eyes, as if she was longing to say something.

"I would want to share my story with you, madam," she said, "but only if you promise me that you won't reveal my name."

"If you say don't, then, of course, I won't! But yes, if I feel that it's a story that others need to hear, then I will write about it in disguise."

"I have to attend a few more houses for repair work now, madam. If you allow me, can I come back in the evening and talk to you?"

"As per your convenience," I said.

It was strange that ever since I had started looking out for stories, I was surrounded by many of them. And why shouldn't that have been? After all, the millions of seconds that we are gifted with in our lives are short but long enough to form beautiful little stories.

It was six in the evening and Siddharth had just returned home from work when the doorbell rang. It was Rohini, still in her formal attire.

"Good evening, madam. I just finished my work so I thought ... I hope I am not disturbing you," she appeared more conscious.

"You aren't, please come in."

As I made her sit in the drawing room again, I had some fear inside me. I was allowing an absolute stranger inside my house, I didn't know what her past was and I didn't know if she was genuine. But then the only way to know more about a story is trust, which was the only thing that always pushed me to go ahead and talk to people despite my insecurities. I had learned to trust from Siddharth.

Despite my irrational behaviour, my anger, my overall negative attitude towards life, he continued to trust me. He continued to believe that this was just a phase; this wasn't the real me. It was his trust that was slowly making me transform into a far better human being.

"Yes, so how have you been?" I started my conversation with her.

She smiled and stayed quiet for some time. "Nice house, ma'am," she complimented.

"Oh, thanks!" I was happy to hear that. "See, I have made those paintings, and this décor in the corner; that lamp was my choice," I flaunted and also tried to divert the conversation a little.

"My childhood wasn't like a regular childhood," she started. "I used to stay in a small town in the Haryana state. My father was a farmer and my mother used to help him on the farm and in the house. The financial status in my house wasn't as great. What do you expect in a farmer's house anyways? I was the third child, the third girl child of my house. Obviously unwanted, who wants a girl child? They can't help the families to earn; one has to get them married, give your hard-earned money as dowry, etc. My mother had three more children after I was born; fortunately, they were all boys, but it had made my mother very weak. Having more children had lead to more responsibility on my father and he ultimately had more mouths to feed. The environment of my family was very negative. My eldest sister was twelve when she ran with her alleged boyfriend from the neighbouring village. She had never told me about her affair and I hadn't seen her boyfriend either, but my father declared that she was characterless and never made any attempt to find her again. A year later, my second sister died in an accident. My mother told me that she had gone to fill some water from the pump on the farm and died due to a bad electric shock. My family didn't seem to be much affected with the loss they had suffered, but I used to cry at nights and miss my sister's presence," she had tears in her eyes and so did I.

"In the coming few months, my family's financial situation was worse than ever. The crops hadn't yielded much and my father had some loan on his head, which used to bother him every day. He used to take that anger out on both my mother and me. While he didn't need any reason to beat or kick my mother, he used to taunt me and slap me for being a girl and being a burden on him every now and then. Once, some people who seemed to belong to a rich family visited my small house. My father appeared different that day. He looked happier.

They got down from their big car and he made them sit on small plastic chairs which he had borrowed from the neighbouring houses. 'This,' he held my hand and brought me to stand in front of them. I was confused. I had no idea what was happening. Amongst the people who sat in front of me was a man in a white shirt and black pants, his moustache was dense and he appeared to have paan filled in his mouth. With him sat a fat lady in a haphazardly draped sari; she was busy examining me from top to bottom. Besides, there were two other men who stood behind them. The man didn't speak, he just nodded, indicated the boys to talk to my father and got up to leave.

'You go with them; you'll have to do whatever work they say. They will take good care of you,' my father took me in a corner and said.

'But where?' I asked. I was very confused.

He slapped me and said, 'Don't shame me by acting smart, I have had enough trouble feeding you. Go quietly and don't misbehave.'

I looked at my mother, she had nothing to say and looked away, I looked around but none of my brothers were nearby. I was barely ten; I had to follow what my father was telling me. Maybe he wants me to work outside the village is all that I could think and left with them."

While Rohini was narrating her story, I was trying hard to control my emotions. I think I knew where this was heading. Thankfully, Siddharth interrupted us with two cups of tea.

"I was making some tea for myself; I thought even you guys would like to have some," he said.

Rohini smiled, got up and said her namaste to Sid. Even I smiled at him; it was adorable how he always used to take care of the little things I needed despite his busy schedule. How many men do that, and do it so selflessly I used to wonder. This short interference lightened up the pressure that was building inside me and I was more receptive to her story now.

"They had taken me to Delhi initially," she started again. "They took me to a house and gave me a small shack-like room to sleep in the first day. The next day, someone woke me up early in the morning, fed me with some tea and biscuits and showed me around the house. I wasn't given any work yet and I was only spoken to by that lady who had initially come to pick me up. I felt she was either constantly examining me or making me more comfortable in that environment. After the lunch hours, she sat with me on the lawn and started asking me bizarre questions. Questions like, do you know how you were born? Do you know what all men need? Do you know why girls are so precious?

I had always known that girls were worthless, that's the way I was brought up. But this lady told me how a girl can increase her worth, how she can polish herself to be a diamond that people want. I hadn't seen or heard about the things that she was telling me then. My naïve mind saw a hope to have a better life with her and I thus blindly followed her instructions and ended up satisfying the burning desire of a relatively older man that night.

She continued to train me more in order to be more desirable, and I took it up as a challenge and blindly followed her instructions in a hope to become the most precious diamond, the one she had told me about. As years passed by, I started facing more difficult men on my bed. Men who used to hurt me on my private parts, men who used to beat me up to feel sexually aroused, men who used to chew my skin, as if I wasn't alive at all. I tried telling this to the lady who had trained me first, but neither she nor anyone else whom I had known along was bothered about anything that I suffered. The more I grew up, the more I started realising that I could never be that diamond that I was told about. Despite people needing me to satisfy their desires, despite me having a roof over my head, I was still unwanted. With time, I also started knowing what family life was, what it was like to have children and what it would mean if someone loved and cared for me, my existence. I started suffocating in my space; I started retaliating to small and big things, I started missing home. I wondered about my sisters. I didn't know if the stories that I heard about them were true. *What if even they were sent off with someone*, I used to wonder. What if even they are silently sobbing in some corner of the country like me? At times I wanted to run, but where could I have run? I didn't have a family; I didn't know any other means to survive. I was scared of the strange world that existed outside the premises where I stayed, outside the bedroom that I worked in."

There was an awkward moment of silence in the room.

"What brought you to Allahabad? Did you manage to gather the strength to run?" I asked her.

She took a long pause and started again, "I didn't run. I could not run. Some big men complained about my attitude to the lady who used to trade me. As the complaints increased more, she said I wasn't meant to be in that city. They needed mellower and softer girls for the clientele they had there and couldn't afford to spread a bad name amongst them. She shifted me to Allahabad. I am sure you must be aware of the area that is infamous for prostitution here and I am also sure you must have never dared to pass near that area. I stayed caged there for many years again."

Rohini was right, I knew about this red light area in the city. Everyone did, in fact, but it was never spoken out loud. I also remembered passing near it one evening and my heartbeat had gone quite up. But though I was scared to pass around it, I had a strong sense of pity for the women whom I thought would be staying there.

"Don't ever stop your car here," my friend had told me once and ever since then I used to wonder what it would be like to survive in a place where I can't even dare to stand for a second.

I remembered a similar place in Hyderabad city where my car had passed once. On that relatively quiet four-lane road surrounded by trees on both sides, I had seen a lady. She was dressed up well in a sari, had some makeup over her face and stood there, partially hiding and peeping from behind a tree. I badly wanted to get down and talk to her. I wanted to ask her from where she got the strength to stand in that quiet and dark place, but I couldn't.

"I had assumed that I was living my destiny and that was my life, but probably miracles do happen," Rohini continued. "The fan in my room was creating constant trouble for many days. One day an electrician from a nearby shop visited to repair it. Since our trader was out for some personal work that day, I had to supervise it and get it repaired myself. The man looked humble, I think he knew what that area was all about, but he still behaved very respectfully with me. That day, it was after many years that I felt respected by someone. I couldn't control my tears in front of him, offered him water and didn't say a word by myself. Somehow he seemed to have understood and spoke to me himself. I don't know why but he could empathise with my pain. Before he left, he showed me how to loosen the wire of the fan. He asked me to do it after a few weeks so that it stops working again. He said he would visit again to repair it, but this time with a plan. With the kind of life I was leading then, I had nothing to lose even if this man turned out to be bad. Thus I decided to trust him. A few weeks later, I did as he had told, and the fan stopped working again. I intentionally did it at a time when the trader was occupied elsewhere. He came again and since nobody suspected him of doing any harm, he carefully managed to take me out of that house. By the time people in that place realised that I was missing, I had travelled to a safer place in the city."

"Nobody came after you? How about that man, didn't they suspect him and catch him?" I asked.

"He sent me off with another man who was waiting on a bike near the building and quickly managed to enter my room again. When the trader came to supervise and asked him where I was, he said he didn't notice because he was busy mending the fan. She couldn't say anything to him because he was an outsider and could have gotten her into trouble. He made me stay in his house for a few weeks till things outside appeared settled, after which," she smiled, "we got married in a temple!"

"Wow! He married you. I want to see him for sure. He has done one of the most daring and noble deeds," I exclaimed.

"His mother was a victim of domestic violence," she told me. "His sister was a victim of an unhappy marriage. One needs to see pain to feel it. One needs to see hardships to become daring. Isn't it, madam?" She smiled.

We parted on that note that day, and on a Sunday that followed that week, she took me to meet her husband as was promised by her. I had taken Sid along; probably I hadn't seen as many hardships as them yet and still couldn't dare to go with them alone.

"You never thought of going to the police and telling them about this place and the activity that runs there?" I asked her husband when I met him.

"Madam, they are running it for years now. They have multiple ways to escape and prove themselves not guilty. I am a small man with minimal contacts; taking this risk will get both of us in trouble. We are happy that we are safe and together, that's it," he explained.

Unlike how our society looks down upon these women, I now knew that they were not where they were by choice. The smile they adorned while they served someone's desire was not the smile of pleasure but a smile of pain. They were someone that had been borne out of a man's need, yet though his need was more acceptable by the society, these poor women were still not. Unfortunately, while we still continued to believe that *men will be men,* these helpless women couldn't even live like normal women. While on our way back, I asked Sid to slow down the car as we passed through that area infamous for prostitution. I could hear some silent screams from behind the walls, some silent cries craving to go home, some silent protests from women who wanted to be free, and some terrible pain which was silent too.

CHAPTER 10

RATNA

A week later from then, I started experiencing some bad abdominal ache. For the first few days, I thought it was due to minor gastric upset and took some self-medication, after which I was worried.

"Sid, I have been unable to drive properly. I am not sure if it's due to exertion. What should we do about it?" I asked him.

"And you're telling me about it now? Five days later. The problem with most women, including you, is that you all are absolutely unbothered about your own health," he looked worried. "We will get an ultrasound done tomorrow morning. Drink a lot of water in the morning and yes, don't eat anything," my doctor husband instructed.

The next morning, I did as he said and went to his hospital with him. Technically, this was supposed to be my first ever hospital visit as a patient. Though I was the first in line for the ultrasound procedure, I was quite impatient for it. The one litre of water that I had drunk in the morning was showing its effects on my bladder.

"There is almost a one-centimetre renal calculus in her ureter, Sid. It's alarming," the radiologist said, looking at the computer screen.

"Congratulations!" Sid looked at me.

"What?" I didn't know what either of them meant.

"Madam, there is a huge stone in your kidney. It has drifted down to a very narrow part of it called the ureter, and you are fortunate that you aren't screaming in pain yet is all I can say," he said.

"Oops!" I said. "So we get some medicine for this?" I asked.

"We get admitted," he kept his hand on my head.

"No!" I made a sad face.

"Yes," he said.

And there I was, fortunate enough to be admitted in a private room of a government hospital, but unfortunate enough to be poked with needles and confined to one corner of a room.

The next few days were troublesome for me. They made me experience many things for the first time in my life. Starting from constant pricks on my hand or arm to anaesthesia that made me unconscious, I saw a very different way life could be. All of a sudden, my empathy for people admitted for long-standing diseases had increased. I could feel the pain of both the patients and the attendants who left everything and stayed with their relatives in the hospitals for uncertain amounts of time. I did have visitors every now and then but it was only Sid who stayed with me all the time. He used to sleep on the sofa-cum-bed in the room at night and attend his duties in the same hospital during the day. Out of all the visitors that I had, one of my aunts who stayed in the same city visited me every day. She made sure to bring home-cooked food for me every afternoon.

"Eat this, you will get well faster," she used to say.

She was a housewife. She used to finish her household work and spend the entire afternoon with me and I loved her presence, it used to comfort me a lot. If she was as busy as the rest of the women around me, even she wouldn't have been available for me, I used to think. I realised we underrate housewives so much! They are the ones who form the background score of our busy lives; it's they who make sure that the daily necessities run smoothly in a man's life. The food is taken care of, the clothes are washed and ironed on time, everything in the house is arranged in perfect shape and order, and yes the biggest of all, they do have time for others. It was sad to think how people still said, *just a housewife!* I wished that our society respected them more and made them felt more needed.

Confined in that room with minimal ventilation for five days after my surgery, I was craving to go out and look at the daylight.

"You will have to stay for two more days and then we will discharge you," the doctor who operated on me told me one morning.

For those next few days though, I requested Sid to take me out of the room so that I could get acclimatised to moving more. One evening, I stepped out of my room;

this was after almost a week. We went to a park within the hospital premises. I looked at the greens like I had never looked at them before.

"The world is so beautiful," I looked at Sid and said. It's strange how we fail to observe the little things around us until we are deprived of them, I thought. Despite being surrounded by all forms of beauty all the time, we are always in pursuit of it. After we came back to our room, Sid sat down with me to have a cup of tea.

The moment we sat someone knocked on the door.

"Sorry to disturb you, sir, but it's a little urgent. Can I talk to you for five minutes?" A lady by the door addressed Sid.

"Oh yes, come in, Ratna. Tell me what happened," he said.

"Sir, I wanted to discuss my child's case with you. He has been admitted for almost eleven days now. This is his file, sir. Is there any possibility to know how many more days it will take?" She appeared humble.

"See Ratna, your child has a severe infection in his liver. Pus has accumulated at many places inside it. We can't say anything till it improves, and even after it does he will need further treatment," Sid explained patiently.

"Sir, I understand," she looked down, "But it's getting very difficult to arrange finances. The everyday bills are taking a toll on me."

"Ratna, your child needs this treatment. If not, he will not survive. Come, sit here," he made her sit on a chair in front of him. "There are certain government officials who are kind enough to give funds for such prolonged treatments. There is also a separate government fund of the hospital where you can submit an application. We can try for both, if either of it works then you will not have to worry about money at all," Sid explained.

"Sir," she folded her hands in front of him, "please let me know what I should do to get these funds. I will do everything possible from my side," she said in a low tone.

"Please don't fold your hands; it's my duty to tell you these things. Wait in the ward. I will ask the billing department to make an estimate of the amount that you may have to spend and have already spent, and then tell you what to do with it."

She thanked him and quietly left the room.

"I don't know how, Tanya, but this lady has been staying here with two of her kids alone for the past eleven days. While one of them is admitted, the other is still a toddler and she has been managing them by herself. Not just that, she herself runs around to get the medicines, food, everything else that is needed. I haven't ever seen anyone else with her at all. No one visits them either."

"Which ward is she in?" I asked him.

"Her child is admitted in the general paediatric ward on the second floor downstairs," he told me.

The next morning, I took Sid's permission to visit that lady in the ward where she was. I visited her around 11 am after the morning rounds were over. The general wards, unlike the private room where I was, were crowded with many more patients in the same big hall. A series of beds lay side by side with one chair per bedside for one relative to sit. The ward smelled of mixed warm odours. I was not sure if it smelled like medicines or the mixed smell of the sweat of so many people in the hall, but I was sure that the smell wasn't pleasant at all. As I looked for bed number six and approached near her, she seemed to look at me in an attempt to recognise me. Though she had seen me the previous night, she hadn't noticed me that well.

"Namaste," I said, "I am Dr Siddharth's wife. I saw you last night when you came up to talk to him."

She immediately got up from her chair, "Sorry, madam, I know I disturbed you in your personal time. I wasn't able to talk to him in the ward in front of so many people, that is why, madam, I am sorry," she folded her hands again.

"You love folding your hands at every little thing I guess," I smiled.

She was surprised to hear that and smiled back in relief.

"I haven't come with any complaint, I have just come here to see you," I said, and she immediately made me sit on the chair and sat on the bed herself. "How is he doing now?" I looked at her child and asked.

"Madam, he talks and giggles on some days and suffers in pain on the rest," she said, patting his hand, while her other toddler played with her sari. "I am just hoping he survives this disease. I don't know who has cursed my child," she started crying.

"Hey! He will be all right. Siddharth told me he would personally try to speak to some authorities for your funds. Don't worry," I assured her and she smiled with that ray of hope.

"Is there no one else that stays with you here?" I asked.

"Madam, this is my family, that's it," she said.

I looked at the vermillion on her forehead and her prominent toe rings.

"My husband isn't dead. He has abandoned us," she said. "We had been married for seven years; technically, we are still married. He runs a small eatery shop in the Pratapgarh town nearby; even I was working with him. When we first got married, he used to own a wheelbarrow and sell nuts. Over the years, I motivated him to start an eatery shop. I cook very well and I can cook fast. Initially, he was reluctant but he used to love the *paranthas* I made at home and thus got convinced to take the risk of starting a shop. I used to make *pakoras, paranthas*, cutlets, Maggi and some other small items along with tea. We used to go and come together and even the kids stayed with us in the shop most of the time. While I cooked, he looked after things to be brought from outside, managed the rent, etc. Madam, it was a decent life that we were leading, wasn't it?" she asked me.

"Of course, more than decent I should say," I said.

"I had even started accumulating money for his education separately," she pointed at her son who lay there with drains and tapes all over his bare abdomen. "He is six now. I had planned to start sending him to school from this year. But then I don't know who cursed us. My husband just lost his mind," she said.

"Usually, we used to come and go home from the shop together, but all of a sudden, he started behaving differently. He used to send the kids and me back home on a rickshaw and come home late at night. Eleven, twelve, once he even returned at two o'clock. He never came home drunk, but he never spoke much either, and always came back and slept. Hc had started ignoring me completely and I used to feel I was staying with an absolute stranger. To add the final ghee in this slow fire, my son fell ill one day. We made many rounds of the hospital in Pratapgarh but nothing seemed to work there. My husband accompanied me to the hospital for the first time, but since the doctors there said that it might be difficult to save my son's life, he started escaping from us entirely. The doctors there advised us to come to this hospital in Allahabad, but I couldn't bring him here immediately because all my savings were exhausted and my husband denied giving me any money for the treatment. I had to keep my child at home and do whatever I could there itself, but it was a mistake; that's where things went worse for my son," she cried again.

"But why did he deny the money?" I was surprised. "Didn't he see his condition himself?" I asked.

"Madam, he had stopped coming home entirely. One day when I lost my patience, I left both my children at home and visited our shop to beg him for my son's health, and there I found another woman with him," she wiped her tears with the *pallu* of her sari.

"Somewhere, I knew that he might be involved with someone else, but I never asked him anything for my children's sake. I knew if I ask him questions about it, he may retaliate and leave me entirely. But, little did I know that he was such a coward, that he wouldn't even stand up for his own children. That lady there didn't allow me to enter my own shop and spoke to me very rudely. I requested her to allow meeting him once for my child's sake but that coward used her as a shield to hide from me. Can you imagine that, madam? I was devastated from inside but I had no time to think about my own feelings. I pushed her aside and saw my husband sitting quietly in a corner of the shop. On seeing me there, he got up in aggression and started speaking random things. He asked me to take my children and do whatever I wanted to and said he wasn't bothered about us anymore. I begged him for money, reminded him how we had started that shop together, and even pleaded him to stay with me till at least my son was better, but I felt as if I was talking to a stone. There was no effect on him at all."

"How could he abandon you just like that?" I was shocked.

"They are men, madam; they can have loose ends, they can be irresponsible and they can run away from anything whenever they want. The society still doesn't question them about it." "How did you land here then?" I asked. "I sold the little gold I had. I am such a fool; I should have done that earlier. The doctors here said if I had brought him here two days prior, the infection would have been less. But in the hope that I had on that man, it never struck me to sell my gold."

The poor lady was still blaming herself for not having thought about selling her gold earlier, I thought.

"I have still been surviving on that money. But, it may exhaust anytime and this time I don't want to take any risk," she kept her hand on his son's head and said.

"What about other members of your family? Why have you not told them about it?" I questioned.

She laughed, "I did," she took a pause. "His parents are cursing me to have given him such a child. They felt it was because of my irresponsibility that my son landed with this disease. As per them, I am an over-ambitious woman who failed to take care of her son and thus I have to bear with it. They have happily accepted his other relationship."

"And your own parents?" I asked.

"As per them, I am living my fate. My father had passed away a few years back and my ailing mother has suffered alone throughout these years. As per her, suffering is nothing but destiny," she was quiet.

The next day was my last day in the hospital. I had mixed feelings. My happiness to get discharged was diluted by thinking about Ratna and people like her who had to be there for longer. That evening, I again went down to the canteen to have tea and on my way found Ratna standing in a corner of the corridor. She was talking over the phone and was crying and shouting at the top of her voice.

"What kind of a man are you? You coward, doesn't it haunt you at night? How are you able to sleep peacefully knowing your own son's state?" She was breathing hard. "You think we can't survive without you? I had stood up with you and given you the strength enough to become something from nothing a few years back. I will now stand strong beside my children, take care of them and make them something worthwhile. You sit, wait and watch." She pressed the buttons of her phone hard from her shivering hands to disconnect the call and stood sobbing quietly in that corner.

The Ratna that I saw today was entirely different from the Ratna that I had met on the previous day. A relatively calmer lady, who said a yes to every responsibility that came her way, was ready to be violent and fight with the world when it came to her child. It was strange how she had killed her own emotions, needs and respect in this process. I was always used to displaying my emotions out loud. I didn't know it was possible to withhold them and kill them as she had. I probably needed to experience motherhood to know what she was feeling then. It's unusual how women can keep their identity aside; sometimes even forget it and take up this beautiful role of givers and caretakers in this otherwise selfish world.

CHAPTER 11

BHAVNA *NANI*

As I met more and more women to unravel womanhood, I ended up tying more knots in my mind instead of having a clearer vision. I had understood each one of them very well, but I was still confused about my own self. Some women that I met had extremely difficult journeys: journeys that I could never relate to. Meeting them did make me feel grateful for my own life, but... weren't my problems entirely different? Wasn't I too sacrificing a lot of things in my life? I could have flown to any portion of the world and explored my maximum potential if I was on the driver's seat of my life. Given an opportunity to work and move the way I wanted to, even I could have turned out to be a Sundar Pichai, I used to think often. It would be wrong to say that I didn't have any control over my life at all because my husband was kind enough to let me take all the important decisions of my life by myself. But, wasn't I still tied? I rather felt more suffocated with my nice man, because it kept me stuck more. Had he been someone like Seema's husband, I too would have had a straightforward reason to walk out of the marriage. Thus, now at this stage after having met so many personas, it was as though I had collected bits and pieces of information but was yet to organise them to derive meaning from it. I now felt the need to meet someone with whom I could discuss this journey of mine, someone, with whom I could talk about my own insecurities, my own life. The good thing was that I knew who this someone was.

"Hey Sid, I am travelling to Delhi tonight," I told him one day.

We had a direct overnight train from Allahabad to Delhi, which was the preferred mode of commute for people from either side. In general also, the train was always my preferred mode of commute since always. Why? I can't say. Maybe because I grew up during a time when flights were still uncommon and were considered a luxury, or maybe because of the childhood memories that I associated with train travel. The entire family in a small coupe, nobody in a hurry to go out and work, surprise small eatables throughout the way, and so on and so forth. Sid dropped me at the station that night, and the next day morning there I was, in the capital city of my proud country! *Beware of people in the station, pay attention to your belongings,* we had been trained well by our mother about the dos and don'ts of the railway station since childhood. Thus, instead of looking right, left or at any other passers-by, I walked fast and walked straight towards the prepaid auto booth on the outside premises of the railway station.

"Govindpuri," I told the man who sat behind the prepaid ticket counter.

He gave me a blue and pink slip, and an auto driver attended me immediately. It was the end of January but the morning was crystal clear, unlike the foggy and smoggy days which otherwise run in the city on most days from

October to almost February each year. New Delhi was always in the news for some or the other reason. But despite the endless fingers pointed at the city for either the increasing pollution or crime, the city had its own charm. The wide and clear roads, the organised metro rail, markets ranging from Khan Market to Sarojini Nagar, something or the other had always kept me minorly attracted towards the city.

"That's it, that cream building, *bhaiya,* I want to go inside the premises of that apartment," I told the auto driver as I approached my destination.

I got down from the auto-rickshaw and looked for the C block elevator; I had beautiful memories with every single thing on that premise, including the sound that the elevator made. I pressed five on the elevator panel and as soon as it stopped and I opened the elevator door, straight in front of my eyes was my Granny's house. Ever attentive as she was even at eighty-three, she stood there smiling from behind the mesh door of her house.

"I hope your train was comfortable," she said as she gave me a warm hug and ushered me inside the house.

Bhavna Nani as we used to call her was my maternal grandmother. Technically she wasn't my mother's mom, but her aunt. I remembered staying at her house at the young age of seven for one entire month during my summer vacations and it was then when I had bonded with her. Since then, I had made sure to visit her house whenever I was in Delhi. The only two people that stayed in her house were she and her husband, my grandfather. Despite the advancements that the country had made I used to still encounter people, including some of my friends, who could not get married to each other just because they belonged to different castes. But these two people who were culturally apart had managed to get married to each other way back, before India's independence. They were the perfect example of love and care for me. I don't know how, but there was a beautiful balance that always existed between their broad opposites. While granny was professionally a doctor, my grandfather dealt in the stock market; while she was a strict vegetarian, he was a Bengali who thrived on fish; while she had quieter ways of dealing with things, he was more vocal and loud. The more I had seen them, the more I had wanted to be like them. But I don't know how I landed myself in the mess that I was living in at that time.

After a quick bath in one of the rooms that she had guided me into, I came out and sat at the dining table with her.

"Here, have some porridge. How would you want the milk? Hot or cold?" She drifted a bowl towards me and asked.

"Hot. I will get it," I got up to get hot milk from the stove, while she nodded and got back to reading her newspaper.

After I ate, we sat in the balcony and I started making some small talk with her.

"*Nani*, for how long have you been with my grandfather now?" I asked her.

She smiled, looked at me in the eye and said, "It feels like eternity!"

I was such a fool to ask that question, I thought.

"It was very challenging for us to set a world of ours together. But I am glad we could," she smiled again.

"Didn't you face problems in adjusting with him after your wedding? I am sure your in-laws would have expected a lot of adjustments from you. I mean, you both were from diverse cultures and I am assuming that the traditions would have been stricter in your times."

"The traditions are always strict, Tanya. Yes, they were at our time too. But ultimately it's about how the two of you attain a balance of thoughts. Why make havoc out of anything? With clarity of thoughts and good communication, things can always be sorted, can't they? He always took a strong stand at points where he thought things could be difficult for me and made them rather flexible. While I indulged in his family and his culture wholeheartedly at whichever points I could. For instance, at his place, there is a small ritual followed by the daughter-in-law, where the newlywed has to cut a portion of uncooked fish which is then cooked and served in the family. I came from a family where we didn't even have an egg. I had never even touched a dead animal, forget cutting it altogether. Your grandfather knew that it would be very traumatic for me and thus having understood that, he was firm about not following that ritual. The family had come up with an alternative way for it. Similarly, I mastered the Bengali language after getting married to him. I brought their grammar books and took it from the start, and today I am extremely proud that I can speak it with so much fluency. Let alone speaking, I am glad I can read the rich Bengali literature in its untranslated version, just the way it was written."

"Oh, yes! Even the clock in the living room has Bengali digits, right?" I asked her.

"Yes, it does. He says I am better than him in speaking Bengali," she laughed.

I couldn't stop adoring her while she spoke.

"*Nani*, I have been extremely confused about womanhood ever since I got married. I feel it's me who has to make all the adjustments. My professional life has gone for a toss. I was so confused about womanhood that I met and spoke to women of various cadre and experiences just to gain, learn and write about them. What many of them have faced is harsh and having seen that, I now have more reasons to rebel."

"Tanya, most of the time, the solution doesn't lie in rebelling against the wrong; it rather lies in accepting and following the right. I have seen times changing many a time in this short life of mine. I feel all of a sudden the wave of rebelling has blown, not just you, but most of the society. It's good to speak up against the wrongs and it's good to fight the bad. But it doesn't mean that we stop acknowledging the good at all. Now that you have met and seen so many women, don't you think womanhood has much graver issues to worry about than just rebelling about the smaller things? Since the times when I was a child to now, we have come a long way ahead. Previously, women used to struggle with health and hygiene alone. Education and independence were farfetched dreams for many and unfortunately, most of them didn't have as many choices as women have now. Now that we have walked some way ahead, our problems are different. We have to work towards them together as a society instead of getting stuck with the smaller individual issues around us. As per me, the most important thing for any woman is whether she is able to make her individual choices. I ask you, are you allowed to make that choice?" she asked me.

"Yes, I am. No one has ever forced me to do anything as such at my husband's house," I said.

She smiled, "At your house, Tanya. If you consider that you belong to a different boat, then how will you two be able to sail together?"

Her statement made me think for some time.

"If you are one of those women who is educated, smart and independent, then instead of getting stuck at being a rebel go out and do whatever you can to uplift other women. If we get stuck in our individual battles, then we won't ever be able to make any concrete changes around us. At the end of the day if we have to make our lives worthwhile, then we have to think of doing something which makes us win as a society. By working selfishly for our own selves, we won't leave anything behind. Isn't it?" She explained.

"You are right and I do understand what you are saying. But how can I do it if I am not satisfied with my own life? I feel even I have the potential to be the CEO of Google. But if I can't even decide the place where I want to settle, then how do you think I can cope up with those thoughts?" I asked her.

"If everyone starts running to become the CEO of Google, then who will take care of the other nooks and corners of the world, my child? I do understand that insecurity of missing out on certain things in life. But always remember, we all occupy a very specific small portion of the big world and the wiser people do the best they can in their specific niches. If we look at farther things and keep running after them, then the race is endless. Mr Pichai would have fought his own battles and just as Google needs him, something else may need you. Being a strong woman doesn't mean running from your family either, Tanya." She smiled again.

I was surprised at the composure that she kept while talking to the restless me. Her words made me think about Meghna's mother-in-law. I could remember how lonely she was when she sat alone in those quarters. I could imagine how lonely she would still be after returning to her hometown. *Nani* was right, if all of us started running then who would stay back, I thought.

"It is extremely unfortunate that a woman is the more ignored of both the sexes in any family," she continued. "She is the one who keeps the entire family knit and makes a beautiful home out of a concrete brick and mortar house. Sadly, she rarely gets the importance she deserves. No matter how educated they are, many women are not able to pursue their careers to the best of their capabilities even today. You know why, Tanya? Because most of them are discouraged from working by people around them. They are told this in various forms, like, *you will be taken care of by the family, it's more important for you to take care of the household now, you have to bear and raise our children, or, why do you want to work so hard?* In a few sad instances, she is asked not to work directly as well."

Just like in Nandini's case, I thought!

"I have also seen instances where the women themselves opt to be dependent on their man. Many of them opt out of their work while they are bearing a child and fail to join back at all. Whatever be the reason, by not being able to work, most of them eventually lose their identities and get stuck with their relationships. "You, Tanya," she looked deep into my eyes, "are someone who is opting out to work by your own self!"

"But ..." I tried to say something but she interrupted,

"I know you would say there are not many options again. But was it not you who had chosen not to work in a corporate company? Is getting employed the only option to work that one has? You can do so much more with your education and calibre. There are so many women around you who need you. Why don't you think of reaching out to them, why don't you think of starting something for them?" She had left me thinking.

By trying to rebel at everything around, I wasn't really heading anywhere. On the contrary, I had filled myself with so much negativity that I couldn't see any possible solutions to my problems at all. Siddharth was the most supportive man anyone could ever have. Despite a beautiful household and a harmonious relationship, I was spoiling things for my own self because of my internal clutter. My anger on the sufferings of women was right but I had to use my capabilities to do something about it, instead of just sitting and just acting rebellious. While I sat there lost in my thoughts, I didn't notice when *Nani* got up and went inside the house. It was only when my grandfather came and peeped in the balcony that I woke up from my thoughts.

"When did you come?" he asked me.

I got up, smiled and replied to his question.

"How was your train journey? I hope you didn't have much trouble in dealing with the rowdy auto drivers at the railway station," he asked.

"Not much, I came home safely," I laughed.

Immediately after my conversation with him, he disappeared into his room, then came back after a few minutes and repeated, "When did you come?"

Nani came and quietly told me that lately he had been suffering from short term memory loss and thus had a habit of forgetting the immediate incidences and conversations.

"He keeps asking the same thing again and again," she murmured.

I sat with him and patiently answered all his questions again.

"We just celebrated our 58th wedding anniversary and look what he gave me for it," *Nani* handed over a greeting card to me and said.

To my beautiful wife, on our anniversary, it read on the outside and had a beautiful big message printed on the inside of it.

"Show me?" *Nanaji* took the card from me and looked at it all over inside out. "Tanya, I know I have this habit of forgetting things nowadays," he said out loud, "but I am certain that I have not given her this card," he said.

"You have," *Nani* heard him, came out of the kitchen and said.

Probably he had spoken that loudly just to make her hear.

"I don't know. I am still not convinced," he said and went back to his room.

Nani laughed, "Actually, I had only purchased this. Each year for the past fifty-eight years, he has always given me a greeting card on our anniversary. This year he had forgotten the date so I bought it on his behalf. If I told him he forgot he would have felt very bad," she smiled. I was speechless at that gesture of theirs.

Later that afternoon, I accompanied *Nani* to her work. Even after her retirement, she was continuing to work for a temple trust hospital. She used to visit there for three hours every afternoon and treat and educate the lesser privileged who came there for free of cost. Throughout her life, she had worked in the capability of a general physician. She had told me that she wanted to specialise in paediatrics, which was children's health, but couldn't do so because her father-in-law had turned severely ill after her wedding.

"My duties at home were more important at that point in time," she had told me.

She hadn't cribbed and cried on her fortune like me, she knew how to set her priorities, and she knew how to move ahead in life with her relations, she knew what being a complete woman meant!

After having gained from all my experiences, I had now started looking at my own life very differently. After I identified my positives, I could see more through each of the stories that I encountered in my journey. Unfortunately, my grandfather passed away in a couple of days from then, and close as he always was to *Nani*, even she joined him somewhere in heaven soon. I opened a foundation for young girls where I now teach them the basics of health, hygiene and safety. Siddharth and a few other doctors collaborated with me too and thus we make sure we provide them with the basic treatments and gynaecological support as well. We also teach them the importance of having their own identities, with a hope that at least the girls who are guided by us would know that they are beautiful and strong beings, who are not meant to be used and mocked upon but are rather meant to be an equal contributor to the society. *Bhavna Girl's Foundation* is what I named the organisation.

Epilogue

Now that I had accepted my life as it was, I was happier and more content. By working positively towards the lives of many other girls, my own life's picture had become clearer. I was now in the process of collaborating with one of my ex-colleagues for developing an app for women's safety. I didn't know how far it would succeed but yes, it was keeping my tech side alive. Moreover, I was not afraid of failures now.

Things had accelerated on the personal front as well; we both had consensually decided to have a child. But well, after we had finished our turn to delay the process, it was now nature's turn to take some time. Thus, it was only after one complete year of persistent trials that I had finally missed one of my regular menstrual cycles. With hope in my heart and doubt in my mind when I had tried to screen for my pregnancy with one of the home test kits available in the market, my heartbeat had gone quite up. The last that I had remembered it going that high was while I was in school and had appeared for my board exams. I was numb after having read the result for my pregnancy. I had this habit of calling Siddharth very frequently to inform him all big and small things, but I hadn't called him that day. It was only after he had returned home later in the evening that I had quietly shown him that strip with two dark purple lines, which indicated that I was pregnant. Further tests and scans had confirmed this in the subsequent days and for the next few months, I harboured a new life inside me.

"That's the head and those are the hands," my gynaecologist had pointed on the scan in one of those appointments, and all I could do was wonder at this marvel of nature.

"I will never be able to feel what you feel now," Sid, who had accompanied me for the scan had said. It was this little statement that had made me realise the power to be a woman.

But as advised by Bhavna *Nani*, I didn't stop working. Neither when I had just conceived, nor when I could deliver anytime. The girls in Bhavna's foundation used to marvel at my ever-growing belly, and I am sure they learned that they could also work when they would have bellies someday.

The day of my delivery was festive. Relatives and friends had crowded up in my tiny hospital room. Flowers, sweets and rattles flooded my side table.

"He looks like a perfect combination of both of you," one of my friends had said, while I carried my few-hours-old boy in my arms.

"While you train the little ladies in Bhavana's foundation about their safety and wellbeing, I assure you that I will train our young man to respect and encourage them," Siddharth said, looking deep into my eyes. "After all, it's both a man and woman who can together conquer and create the much-needed differences in our society."

I smiled.

Printed in Great Britain
by Amazon